Praise for THE KING OF AVERAGE

"A skilled and witty tale about a boy who would be king that should appeal to children and adults."

"This is a volume that kids and parents can read together because it works on two levels—young ones should love the adventure-packed plot and hilarious characters, and grown-ups should chuckle at the wordplay embedded in every page. Schwartz's characters are more than clever—they're ingenious."

"Schwartz's nicely succinct writing style places the focus on the striking worlds he creates. The book delivers an important lesson—be your own hero. With this debut, the author should soon be a hero to readers everywhere."

—KIRKUS REVIEW

"THE KING OF AVERAGE is a unique fantasy with a powerfully encouraging message for youth."

—IndieReader

"Gary Schwartz's The King of Average is engaging, imaginative, entertaining and funny while also exploring real emotional depths. It's like reading a lost work of L. Frank Baum."

—Brian McDonald author of
Invisible Ink and *The Golden Theme*

"The King of Average" by Gary Schwartz is a hilarious, adventure-packed, epic journey to find self-worth. As thoroughly 'kid friendly' as it is consistently entertaining... Highly recommended for school and community library children's fiction collections.

—Midwest Book Review

"Gary Schwartz has written a book for all young people, but especially for those who have slipped between the cracks in their homes or communities. He takes an emotionally neglected child through an incredible journey that introduces him to his true self."

—Jonice Webb, PhD., author of Running on Empty: Overcome Your Childhood Emotional Neglect

"This delightful, pun-filled allegory tells the story of a neglected boy who is convinced that he has no worth. Inspired to become the King of Average, he undertakes a journey to a fantasy land filled with interesting characters that have strong personalities despite also being archetypes. Inspired by The Phantom Tollbooth—but not derivative—the book is fast-moving and funny, with a touch of sadness. It will appeal to adults as much as YA readers, reminding all that average is not easy since everyone is special in his or her own way.

—BookLife Prize for Fiction

THE KING OF
AVERAGE

GARY SCHWARTZ

Cover Designer: Gwen Gades
Interior Layout Design by Vanya Drumchiyska at Polish & Publish
Edited by Christina Lepre

Previously published by Booktrope Editions, 2015

This is a work of fiction. Names, characters, places, brands, media, and incidents are either the product of the author's imagination or are used fictitiously. Any resemblance to similarly named places or to persons living or deceased is unintentional.

Published by Bunny Moon Enterprises, LLC.
PRINT ISBN: 978-0-9975860-7-7
HARDCOVER ISBN: 978-0-9975860-2-2
EBOOK ISBN: 978-0-9975860-0-8
Library of Congress Control Number: 2015916003

For my mother and father, who did the best they could.

Map of Average

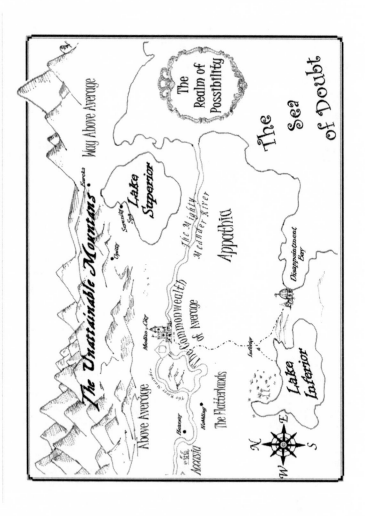

Table of Contents

CHAPTER 1

Just James

JAMES WAS NOTHING special: just a typical eleven-year-old boy. Who cared if he was an only child? No one. Who cared if he had no friends? Nobody. Was it his fault his father had left when he was a baby? Yes. According to his mother, James had caused all her troubles. "Oh, how I wish you were never born!" she'd moan. He didn't mean to make her so miserable, but what could he do? That's just who he was.

If there was one word you could use to describe James, it was "nice." That's if you noticed him at all. He acted nice even when he didn't have to—by himself in his room, just for practice.

No one had any cause to give James a second thought and that's the way he liked it.

At school, he constantly doodled in his notebook. He doodled only one thing: rolling hills with an ever-narrowing, winding road cutting through halfway down the page and disappearing at the horizon line just below some big triangular mountains. It was a perspective drawing he had learned to do in art class. He wasn't good at drawing people (though he tried), and he wasn't interested in drawing cool cars like some of the other boys. And he *definitely* wasn't interested in drawing horses. (That was a girl thing.) He just liked to doodle this image for no particular reason.

It was the end of the quarter at school, and James was at his desk in homeroom, head down in his notebook, doodling, while Mrs. Decker strode up and down the aisles passing out report cards. "These need to be signed and turned back in tomorrow."

James ran down his list of grades. Math: C-, Science: C-, Social Studies: C, Art: C, English: C+, French: C+, Reading: C+. *James does not apply himself. Could do much better*, read the teacher's comment in red ink. *Conference requested*. That's not good, James thought.

When he got home, his mother was already in her bathrobe and on the phone with Sadie, their next-door neighbor. Sadie was the only one who would listen to his mother's complaints, probably because she liked to complain as much as his mother did.

His mother's white uniform from the Manor House Diner hung over the red vinyl chair by the secondhand red formica table where she sat. That's where James would sit when she served him his dinner of unwanted sandwiches and other leftover items from the restaurant. She didn't like to cook.

James watched her light another cigarette while absently stirring her coffee, keeping the phone pressed between her ear and shoulder. The table was littered with dirty dishes and papers. The large square glass ashtray brimmed with cigarette butts.

"Uh huh, me too…"

"If that was me, I'd—uh huh."

"I know what you mean. I... I'd—uh huh."

She didn't really want to hear Sadie complain; she was looking for an opening to vent her own frustrations.

James patiently stood nearby holding the report card, waiting for her to notice him. When she finally did, she made a shooing motion, mouthing the words, "Go upstairs." When he didn't move, she covered the mouthpiece and hissed at him, "Don't you have anything better to do?" He handed her his report card. She barely scanned it.

"I don't have time for a conference. Tell her I work all day. This is the best you can do? You can't do anything right, can you?"

"Could you sign it? Please?"

She took a long drag on her cigarette, exhaled, and squinted to keep the smoke from getting in her eyes.

She put the report card on top of the folded newspaper next to the overloaded ashtray. And, still cradling the phone on her shoulder, she stubbed out her cigarette, grabbed a pencil, and quickly scribbled her name on the report card.

"Why did I ever have children, Sadie? Why am I so cursed?"

She lit another cigarette.

"What? Nothing. Just my son. A scholar he's not. Just like his father, the good-for-nothing bum!"

Like my father, James thought. Even a good-for-nothing bum like him couldn't stand me. His dad must have been a bum to saddle his mother with him. James had an urge to protest but didn't want to set her off. She had an awful temper.

When she got to ranting at him for ruining her whole life, he'd retreat to his room and wait for things to calm down.

He'd imagine arguing back, "I'm not so bad. Okay, so I'm not the world's greatest son... but I'm definitely not the worst!" There were worse kids—lots worse! Bobby Jenner, for example: a brooding bully who lived up the street. He picked on everyone on the block littler than he was and pounded them every chance he got. Last year, he had set his own house on fire. That was one rotten kid.

I could never be that bad, James thought as he looked at the report card. And I'm not that dumb either, he insisted to himself. I didn't even fail one subject. Not one!

CHAPTER 2

The Great Idea

ON HIS WALK HOME the next day, James took his usual shortcut, cutting across Mrs. Shubin's backyard toward Hillside Avenue. He considered his report card. All C's. C stands for satisfactory, he told himself. It means average. You could get by with all C's.

"See? I'm not so terrible!" he said aloud. He glanced around. Had anyone heard him? No. The only living thing in sight was a little blackbird with orange-tipped wings perched on the telephone wire above his head.

It was a relief to finally hear it out loud. "So I'm average! What's wrong with that?! Absolutely nothing!" Then it came to him, an idea so intriguing and paradoxical that he had to laugh. What if I was more average than anybody else in the entire world?!

He was very pleased with himself for coming up with such a wonderful idea. It made him smile as he walked. The more he thought about it, the better he felt. All C's! That's average intelligence. Physically, he was average too. When he stood in line at school in order of height, he was always right in the middle. And he was never picked last for team games, like Todd Grant, who couldn't play very much because he was small and had asthma. Even his name—

James. Probably the most common name in the history of the English language. "I bet I could become the most average person who ever lived!" he announced.

That's when the little bird dove from the wire and headed straight for his head. "Wraawk! You could!" it cawed.

James covered his head with his arms as the bird dove at him again squawking, "It's possible!" Then it took off like a shot and disappeared.

Did that bird actually speak? James thought. Maybe it was a mynah bird or something.

He started back for home but stopped when he spied another strange thing: a gray goat wearing wire-rimmed spectacles and a green tweed vest stood in Mrs. Shubin's garden, calmly grazing on some pansies. A real live goat! The neighborhood had its share of dogs and cats, but never any farm animals. Especially ones in fancy clothes.

Not wanting to scare the goat, James edged closer, moving slowly, until he heard it mutter, "Oh, me. Oh, dear me. Dear mee-ee-ee!"

James blinked. Then blinked again—hard. "Are you a real goat, or someone dressed up to look like a goat?" The little goat offered its backside to him. Cautiously, James reached down and patted the goat on its bony rump. "You're a real goat, all right."

"Go ahead, kick me!" The goat shook its head, pansy petals flying from his mouth. "It's all my fault! We're doomed! Baaaaa!! Ba-aaaaaa!" It nudged its rump against James's leg. "Go on! I can take it!"

"What are you talking about? What's your fault? And how can a goat talk, anyway?!" James scanned the yard. "Is someone hiding somewhere doing your voice? A ventriloquist or something? Is this some kind of joke? Hey! Who's doing this?!"

The goat looked directly at him. "My, my, my! Suspicious, aren't we?"

James rubbed his eyes. "This can't be real."

"Oh, but it is, James. It is real," the goat assured him. James couldn't speak.

"Oh, dear! What a fool I am. How thoughtless of me. Let me introduce myself, I am Mayor Culpa."

"M-Mayor Culpa? Mayor of what?" James asked, finding his voice at last.

"It's an honorary title," said the goat. "I am the royal mascot of Average. And you are James, an average boy. Am I right?"

"H-h-how do you know m-m-my name?" James stammered, more than a little discombobulated.

"A little bird told me-ee-e."

"Ha, ha, very funny. I'm on TV, aren't I?" He looked around for the hidden camera.

"Enough! No more questions! Follow me-ee-e!" The goat took off toward the well-worn path by the lilac bushes.

What was a talking goat doing wearing clothes and spectacles? Maybe there was a circus or carnival in town.

James wondered if he might be coming down with some kind of virus. Perhaps he had eaten something that made him hallucinate. Or maybe he was just going nuts. Whatever the reason, he watched the goat disappear into the hedge and bolted after it.

CHAPTER 3

The Realm of Possibility

JAMES HADN'T GONE more than a few steps before something even more unbelievable happened.

He was no longer in Mrs. Shubin's backyard. The familiar houses were gone. In fact, there *were* no houses, just a rolling grass-green plain. Craggy mountains wreathed in mist and clouds rimmed an endless horizon. No transporter beam had disassembled James's molecules and reassembled them on another planet. Somehow, in a flicker of an instant, everything had changed.

James froze. The goat trotted back.

"What's the matter now?"

"Where am I?"

"You're here and we're he-ea-aded to Average."

James hardly heard a word the goat said. He was still grappling with what had just happened. How had he gotten here? And where is "here"?

"Step lively, there's no-oo time to lose. Our king is gone—vanished!"

"What are you talking about?"

The little goat kept on as if it hadn't heard. "And it's all my fault! Baaa-aaa-aah!"

When he saw James gaping at him and not moving, the goat stopped wallowing in guilt for a moment and smiled (as much as a goat could smile).

"Ah! Good! Yes, yes, very good indeed. Of course, it's to be expected. The average person doesn't catch on too quickly. Let me explain. And try not to ask too many questions; there's only so much an average person should know."

"H-H-How…?" James stammered.

"How did you get here? The usual way. Nothing unusual ever happens in Average, only ordinary things. It's the law!"

"Only ordinary things," James repeated.

"Not grasping it right away," the goat nodded approvingly. "Fine. I'll go a little slower. You… are… not… far…from…Average. The Kingdom of Average, to be precise. A Commonwealth in the Realm of Possibility."

The goat waited patiently for James to digest this before continuing.

"I'm told you want to become the most average person in the world. Is that correct?"

"How did you hear that?"

"Like I said, a little bird told me-ee-e."

James shook his head vigorously, trying to rattle his brain into sanity. There were no signs of his neighborhood anywhere. Instead, he surveyed a landscape very much like the one in his doodles. Only this wasn't crayon, ink, or pencil. The sky was real, cloudless, and pale blue; the air was still; and the ground smelled of real earth and greenery. This was real. Very real! Stands of small trees dotted the rolling plain in the distance. Each looked to be a day's walk away.

He looked right and left for anything resembling his old neighborhood, but there was nothing. Not a house, fence, garden, or path. Farther out, more rolling hills swelled and behind them, far off in the distance, stood jagged mountains shrouded in a gray haze.

"We-ell-ll?"

The Realm of Possibility spread out before him. It was stunning and totally beyond belief.

"I'm imagining all this. Aren't I?" He took a deep breath and looked about. "I have to get home. How do I get out of here?"

"Give up now and go home if you want. We don't abide failure," warned the goat.

James's mind kept reeling. He shook his head harder, trying desperately to shake this reality away without success.

"Hmmm. You don't look very bright standing there with your mouth open. Maybe you're not as average as I was led to believe. But if you really aspire to be truly average, then follow me."

James took another deep breath and steadied himself.

"Are you average or not?" asked the goat.

"I'm average all right... or, could be—" But before he could say anything more, the little goat took off.

James called after him, "Wait! I'm coming with you." He quickly caught up and marched alongside the goat. "Okay, okay. I can't deny I'm actually here. This is so weird. It feels like it's really happening. I'll probably wake up or come to eventually," he said, trying to sound as nonchalant as he could, though that was the furthest thing from what he was feeling. This was the most fantastic thing that ever happened to him and he honestly hoped it *was* real.

"Besides," he said, attempting to sound rational, "if I really am going to be completely average, I should see what Average looks like, shouldn't I? What's it like? Nice, I expect."

"It's not a bad place. Goo-o-ood as some, not as good as others," said the goat. "Some places are baaa-aa-d. Take Accusia. There's always such turmoil there and they constantly blame us for it. Below Average is Apathia. Nothing ever goes on there to bother about, for the most part. Not so bad, I suppose, but who cares? Then there are the places above Average in the highlands on the other side of Expect Station, where we are now. No one from Average ever goes there if they can help it. And wa-aay in the distance over there— it's hard to make them out they're so far away—are the Unattainables, the highest mountain range in the world. Its highest peak is Mount Impossible. Beyond that, they say, is the Realm of Genius. No one really knows if it exists. Many think it's a myth. But there are stories."

"Uh-huh," was all James could muster.

"Never mind all that. We have enough to deal with right here. Our king has gone missing! Everything was just fine and then he vanished without so much as a word."

"So you had a king and now he's gone," James repeated.

"O-oh-oh, he was such an average king!" the goat rhapsodized. "So wonderfully mediocre!"

James nodded as if he understood, but truth be told, he didn't. "What did he do to be so average?"

"Nothing we didn't expect," the goat sighed. "Now he's gone and there's no one to rule Average."

"What about you? You're a mayor... Couldn't you—?"

"Me-ee-eee-e, King of Average? I'm a goat! Too strange. It's not permitted."

"I guess you need someone human. That sounds logical," James agreed.

"Not just *someone*! We need the most average person in the world. Someone completely, absolutely, perfectly average in every way. Someone like you."

"Me? You think I'm average enough to be the king?"

"That remains to be see-een."

The goat stepped up his pace. "If Average can't maintain its place in the world, there'll be nothing for the world to compare itself to. Disaster!" he called out over his shoulder toward James as he trotted along. "Hurry! I must present you to the Council of Judges in Median City."

"The Council of Judges?" James had to jog to keep up.

"Yes, the...judges," panted the goat. "They deal... in... the Law of Averages. They gave...me a 67 percent chance... of finding you," he huffed. "They also said...there was a slight chance... you wouldn't come. Less than 10 percent... But you did, thank goodness."

The idea of being so important gave James pause. "A... king? I... don't know..." James said between gulps of air as he jogged along. He wasn't a very fast runner.

The goat stopped abruptly and turned to James.

"You are the only eligible candidate! You can't refuse. If you do, we will fail! We'll be ruined, and it'll be all my fault."

The goat's expression changed from mild anxiety to awe at the enormity of being blamed for the collapse of an entire kingdom. He pawed the ground and stamped his hooves in a fit of recrimination.

James tried to calm the goat. "I don't see how this could all be *your* fault."

"It is my fault and always will be!" snapped the goat. "I'm a Scapegoat and proud of it."

"A scapegoat?"

"As long as I'm to blame, no one else can be burdened. It's what I was bred for."

"Do you mean nothing can ever be my fault?" James asked.

"Of course! You leave that to me," the little goat snorted, peevishly. "May I continue?"

As Culpa went on explaining, James wondered what it would be like to be king. What do kings actually do? Maybe, if I wasn't leading armies and fighting battles, I would just sit on the throne all day granting or not granting requests. Maybe I'd decree something or other—

"You're not paying attention!" scolded Culpa.

"I'm sorry," said James.

"No! My fault entirely. Perfectly all right," said the mayor. "A perfectly normal thing to do. You are, after all, average and the average person can't pay attention to any one thing too long. That is, after all, exactly what we need. Fine!" The goat bowed his head and muttered to himself, "Probably bored you with too many details."

Culpa trotted over to a nearby tree and butted his head against it. He rammed it several times with loud thwacks and thuds, punctuating each word with a head-butt. "Boring!" *Thud.* "Stupid!" *Bang.* "Story!" *Thwack.* Finally, he stopped. "Much better!"

"Sorry," James replied.

"No need to apologize," said the scapegoat cheerfully. "Not your fault."

"Doesn't it hurt when you butt your head like that?"

"Of course," Culpa replied. "Not to worry though, I can take it."

They continued on at a half-trot.

"Is it far to Median City?" James asked after a while, breaking the silence. "Not too far."

"How far?"

"Just far enough."

Even at this pace, James was running out of steam and patience. "Why won't you give me a definitive answer?"

"That's enough of that!" snapped the goat. "You ask too many questions! You don't need to know everything. That would make you a know-it-all. And that is *not* average! Too many questions require too many answers and I don't have them. No one in Average has all the answers, or needs them, for that matter."

James saw his point. If one were to be completely average one would have to ask just the right amount of questions. But how many was that?

CHAPTER 4

The River Maunder

AFTER AN HOUR of steady walking they came to the edge
of a river. James and Culpa took long, satisfying drinks and
sat by the bank. James dangled his feet over the edge,
brushing the water with the toe of his sneaker. He took a
rock and threw it into the water and watched the ripples
move out from where the rock went kerplunk. James sat
there happily, thinking about ripples; how one always leads
to another and another.

Suddenly, they heard a voice coming from the tall brown
wheatgrass on the far bank of the river. "Shhhhhh. They'll
hear us!"

It was a high-pitched, wheedling whisper—a cross
between a whine and nails on a blackboard. "We can hear
you!" James called out.

James and Culpa listened to the odd debate coming from
a clump of grassy weeds and cattails.

"But *mon ami*, 'zey are most likely friendly and may even
be rich! 'Zey could benefit us enormously!" It was a
boisterous, pleasant voice speaking in what James recognized
as a French accent.

"They're thieves with knives! They're going to rob us, I
just know it! We remind them of someone they hate! They
want revenge!" replied the irritating voice, quavering with
fear. It didn't have an accent. Then he heard it whine

unintelligibly, raspy and shrill. The whine had a squeaky quality, like a slightly bent wheel on a bicycle.

A dapper, rotund man in a beige suit emerged from the rushes, fanning himself with a brown bowler hat.

"*Zut alors!* We are found out! Heh, heh! 'Allo, *mes amis!* Yoo-hoo!"

His shiny black mustache was well groomed and thin. It was tightly wound and waxed at the ends, so much so that it looked like checkmarks framing the man's long nose. He had a monocle wedged in one eye above his rosy cheek. It was attached by a ribbon to his lapel. He sported a red necktie and wore a light brown brocade vest, the fabric pulling at the buttons so tightly it seemed ready to burst.

In his vest pocket, a place usually reserved for a pocket watch and chain, a tiny, pale, bald-headed man peeked out. He squinted and squirmed. His long bulbous nose dangled over the edge of the pocket like a very short trunk.

"Yoo-hoo!" the Frenchman called out again, smiling broadly. He swept the grass out of the way with a wave of his gold-tipped walking stick. "'Allo! 'Eere we are! Peek-a-boo-oo, we see you!"

James waved back. "Are you lost?"

The man laughed, "No, no, no, not at all!!" while simultaneously, the little man in his pocket shrieked, "Yes, yes we are! Totally lost!"

"Please. Ignore my little friend. 'Ee's a little touchy today. Ah! What a glorious day, *n'est-ce pas*?"

"Yes, it is!" replied James, recognizing the phrase from French class. It meant "is it not so?" It sounded like "nest pa" and that's how James remembered it—a father bird in his nest.

"Terrible day!" the little man in the pocket insisted. "Awful!"

James thought maybe the Frenchman was a ventriloquist, because he never saw the little man's mouth move. It was a small frown, pinched and puckered, hidden behind his thick nose and the pocket's rim.

Culpa eyed the strange pair suspiciously.

The larger man smiled and waved once more, silently nodding and tipping his bowler hat. He surveyed the river and his surroundings and looked up at the sky in utter admiration.

"Let's see what they want," James suggested as he rolled up his pants and removed his sneakers and socks. He stuffed his socks in the sneakers and tied the laces together, hung them around his neck, and waded into the river.

"Jaa-aam-ess! Wait!" Culpa cried.

The river suddenly churned. As the current pulled at James, he felt as if he were going to be swept away.

"Whoa! Oohhhh!" The water rushed around his legs, tugging and pushing. With considerable effort, he managed to leap back onto shore.

"I should have warned you," Culpa said regretfully. "If you had drowned, it would have been my fault and I would have felt terrible. I wouldn't have been able to live with myself!"

"Well I didn't drown, okay?" James cut him off. "This constant blaming yourself for everything is getting annoying."

"You're right. I'm sorry…" the goat said, looking around for a tree to ram.

"It's my own fault!" James admitted.

"Oh, no! NO! James! NEVER! It's entirely my fault, please!"

"Okay, okay—it's your fault, if that makes you happy," James said, turning his attention to the water. "What happened to the river, anyway? It was calm and shallow just a second ago."

"It's the River Maunder, a tributary of the mighty Meander. You can't just cross it. It gets angry if you do. You've heard the expression 'Don't cross me or you'll regret it?' Well, it started with this river."

"So how do we get across?" James asked.

"By not wanting to," replied the goat.

"I don't understand."

The goat smiled in a self-satisfeid way. "The bird was right—you're the perfect candidate."

"Who—" James stopped himself, fearing he might be too inquisitive.

"The river will let you across as long as it feels it isn't being crossed. Just play lazily in the water, dawdle, and waste enough time; eventually, you'll get to the other side."

"What do you do if you're in a hurry?"

"Drown."

Culpa went on, "The Meander and the Maunder are the borders between Average and Expectation. To enter Average, you have to waste time; the more the better. The river hates it when you have a goal or deadline. Having a very specific goal is uncommon in Average," lectured the goat. "And now, because we have someplace to be, we're stuck. Baa-aaa-aaaa! We're going to be too late. This is not an average situation. I-I don't know what to do-ooo-oo," he whined.

"If I fail I'll be exiled, and I'll deserve it, too! Baa-aah-aah-aaa!"

James had an idea. "I'm not sure I really want to get there on time anyway," he said loudly to Culpa with a wink, signaling for him to play along.

"Can I ride you into the water and just splash around awhile? It'll be fun!" He waved to the pair on the other side of the river, giving them a big smile and an encouraging nod. The Frenchman returned the wave and smiled back, acknowledging them with a raise of his walking stick.

"Ride on me?" The mayor stiffened.

James nodded and winked again, this time more pronouncedly. Then the goat smiled and nodded, seeing what James was up to.

"Of course!" said Culpa in an over-loud voice for the river's benefit. "Why not? We have nothing better to doo-oo!"

So saying, the mayor pushed his head through James's legs and hoisted him up onto his bony back with an "oof."

"Giddyap!" said James.

"What's 'giddyap'?" asked the mayor.

"It's how we tell animals to get a move on where I come from," explained James.

"Oh," said the mayor. "We just say 'let's go.'"

"Well, let's go, then," said James, urging the goat forward.

They waded into the calm green-blue water.

Kerploosh. James sat atop the goat, firmly gripping the collar of Culpa's vest, and splashed the water with his bare feet.

"Whoopee tai aye yay!!" yelled James, playfully kicking water in the face of the patient goat. "Let's have some fun!" he shouted, raising his voice for the river's benefit. The mayor shook off the water with a shudder of his head that vibrated down his whole body, nearly unseating his rider.

"'Ooray! *C'est magnifique!* Marvelous! Look at the goatsmanship he displays! Quite impressive, eh?" the Frenchman cheered.

"Leave me out of it!" squeaked the sour little man in his pocket.

"Now what? Should we go fishing?" James mused. "Or we could take a swim. There's just *so* much we can do in the water." Culpa waded in farther with James still astride as the river lowered to a trickle.

"Baaa-aaah-aa," replied the goat, reverting to his native tongue.

James leaned down near Culpa's ear. "We're almost there!" Then he shouted, "Giddyap—I mean, let's go!"

But James had misjudged the distance. The river began to rise and the current strengthened. The goat struggled to keep his footing and then suddenly he was lifted off the river bottom.

Quickly, James reached up and grabbed the end of a low-hanging branch to avoid being swept downstream. He hooked his legs under the belly of the goat to keep them from being separated. Culpa began treading water, bleating piteously.

"*Sacre bleu!* 'Zey are real daredevils! 'Zey must be champion swimmers, non?" said the Frenchman, admiringly.

"No!" said the little man in his pocket. "They're going to drown…. Let's get going before people think we did it!"

The Frenchman clapped and cheered, "'Ooray!"

James clung to the branch with both hands, clutching the goat between his legs while the river churned white foam, becoming a furious, roaring torrent.

"Hang on, Mayor Culpa!" James hollered.

"No, no! Let me go, I did this to us! Save yourself! I wouldn't blame you if you did. It'll teach me a good lesson!"

There was no time to answer. Although he had never succeeded in doing even one pull-up in gym class, James strained to pull himself and the goat up onto the branch and out of the water. But he could only hang there. He tightened his grip around the goat's midsection and managed to hoist him up as high as he could. They were both clear of the raging river, hanging onto the branch, dangling precariously above the water.

"Amazing!" the Frenchman said. He looked on in wonder at the sight of James hanging from a tree limb with the soggy goat hooked between his legs.

"Not bad," admitted the little man grudgingly.

"Let me go-o-o! Save yourself!" the goat pleaded.

James strained to pull himself up but couldn't manage it. The water continued to rise. It was now at his knees and up to the shoulders of Culpa, who bleated wretchedly.

"I don't think I can do it!" James wailed, angry at himself for being such a weakling.

Overhead a thick gray cloud materialized, drifting slowly down toward the worsening crisis. It cast an ominous shadow that crept toward them.

The Frenchman hollered encouragement. "You can do it! I am sure!"

"Didn't you hear him? He said he can't!" the little man contradicted. "Let's get outta here!"

The Shadow separated from the cloud and leapt at them from the riverbank. The sky darkened and James lost sight of the shore. He was surprised to find himself on the verge of tears. Hanging from a branch with a talking goat between his legs and a strange Frenchman cheering him on over a dangerously roaring river was no time to cry. James hung on for a few more seconds, feeling very sorry for himself.

A dark despair came over him. "What's the use?" he cried, giving up and falling into the water with Culpa—but only up to their knees!

Upon hearing him declare defeat, the river had instantly receded.

James picked himself up and stood on the riverbed, sopping wet. Culpa shook off the water. James watched the dark cloud dissipate and retreat, but the gloomy Shadow lingered a moment before following after it. *That's odd,* James thought, *a shadow can't—*

"'Zat was 'ze most amazing, daring thing I have ever seen, saving 'zat poor little goat. I salute you! 'Ooray! What courage! What bravery!"

James weakly smiled an acknowledgement but knew his success had been a combination of his inept weakness and dumb luck. But there was no time to wallow in self-pity because the scapegoat was wailing so loudly. "I'm so-oorry, James. I dragged you dow—"

James quickly realized that they were still standing in the drained riverbed, and he yanked Culpa up by the collar and dove for the other side, dragging the surprised goat with him. The river immediately began to rise, but by the time the current reached them, they were safe on the other side of the River Maunder.

CHAPTER 5

The Optimist and the Pessimist

JAMES SAT on the bank and collected himself, putting on his shoes and socks. He leaned over to the goat and whispered, "Do you know them?"

"Oh, *mon Dieu!*" exclaimed the Frenchman, overhearing him. "'Ow utterly uncouth! *Pardonnez moi!*" Jumping to his feet, he proffered a small white card engraved in very fancy script: *Monsieur W. Roget, Optimist.*

Mayor Culpa strained to read the card. "Roget?" he said, pronouncing it with a hard 'G' and a hard 'T.' "Optometrist?"

James had only gotten a "C" in French but knew how to pronounce the man's name properly. "It's pronounced *Ro-zhay.* And he's an optimist, not an optometrist."

The little goat frowned, worried James might be above average somehow.

"Exactly! I am Monsieur William Roget! And 'zis is my partner, Kiljoy," the Frenchman said, referring to his vest pocket. "Pessimist-at-large."

"At *large*! What a joke!" sneered the little man. "Look at me! I'm tiny and I'm stuck with you and I can't do a thing about it."

Kiljoy eyed James suspiciously and nodded a tentative hello, his nose hanging between his bony fingers.

"This is Mayor Culpa, and I'm James."

"Contender to the throne of Average!" Culpa said with his nose in the air, trying to sound official.

"My, my," said Monsieur Roget. "Impressive. Royalty? Is 'zis true? I 'ave never met a king before."

"And I've never met a professional optimist. You do that for a living?"

"Absolutely!" said Roget. "'Ze amateur optimist looks at things only one way. On 'ze bright side, of course. But, when he sees a glass of water filled halfway, a traditional optimist sees it as only 'alf full. But a *professional* optimist is also happy to see fresh, clear water to drink or wash with or to water plants and make things grow. Like food for instance! 'Alf-full or 'alf-empty? For amateurs!"

He stood there proudly, clasping the lapel of his brocade vest in a pose that reminded James of the famous portrait of Napoleon he had seen in a history book.

James noticed Kiljoy rolling his eyes, having probably heard this speech a million times. The tiny man slapped his forehead in resignation and slid down into his pocket.

"Come on!" bleated Culpa. "It's getting dark, we're very late. It's not good to keep the council waiting to-oo-o, too long."

"It's like I'm in some bizarre version of *Alice in Wonderland*! 'I'm late, I'm late! For a very important date...,'" said James, doing his best impression of the White Rabbit.

Culpa looked shocked. "Sarcasm is against the law in Average. It's a tool of the inferior man of superior intelligence and not a trait of an average person."

"I was just making a joke."

"Oh! A joke, yes? Of course! *Oui*, a good one! *Non?*" cried Roget, slapping James on the back, who didn't quite get it but laughed heartily nonetheless. He abruptly stopped and drew James close and whispered confidentially, "Er, Monsieur James, would you mind if we come with you? Kiljoy and I were touring the countryside looking for adventure. We crossed 'ze river some time ago from Dullsville. It is a nice enough place, *oui*. But frankly, very boring. And then, you came along! I would enjoy it immensely if we could, er... ah... tag along?"

James looked to Culpa, who didn't object. James considered it. Normally he kept to himself, not because he much liked being alone but because of how his mom would react if he imposed any sort of friend or playmate on her. He could just imagine how she'd take this strange bunch. Besides, this optimist seemed a jolly sort and would probably find something nice to say about even the worst things.

"Sure," said James.

Culpa was already pulling at his sleeve, urging him along. Roget and Kiljoy fell in alongside them.

The way to Average was a trail of beaten-down grass, which led to a well-traveled dirt path. The scenery reminded James again of his doodle, rolling hills with a road cutting through to the horizon. They climbed a small hill and saw a walled city perched on the horizon.

"There it is. Median City. Jump onto my back!" ordered the mayor. "You too, Mon-sewer. I haven't got all day!"

"How much of 'ze day 'ave you got?"

Culpa snorted as James and Roget climbed onto his back. Once they were safely mounted, the goat trotted along at a quick pace.

Kiljoy moaned and protested with every bump and lurch. "Watch where you're going! We'll fall off and break something!"

James pleaded with Culpa in between "oofs" every time his bottom hit the goat's bony back. "Let us... *oof*... get off... *oof*... your back! *Oof*... Ple-ee-ee-ease! ... *oof*... It's too much for you-u-u!"

"I ca-aan take it!" the scapegoat assured them.

CHAPTER 6

The Nervous Nellies

"WHAT'S GOING TO HAPPEN when we get to Median City?" James asked.

"The council will test you for your suitability," said Culpa.

"I hate tests!" said James.

"Very typical," the goat nodded approvingly.

But that did little to make James feel better. His mother's words echoed in his head. *You can't do anything right, can you?* His heart sank, and he sighed.

Culpa trotted on and out into a large field dotted with clusters of bushes. The gentle rolling terrain made the ride atop the goat a little less bouncy.

"Yaaaaaaaaaaaaaaaaaaaaaa! Whoooop! Whooop! Get 'em!" cried a voice from behind a thorny hedge.

"YEEEEEE! YAAAAAAW! YIPES! WAAAAAAAGH!"

A horde of voices rang out over the field. Thirty or forty scrawny, bare-chested, pasty pink little men, knee-high to James, scrambled out from behind a nearby thicket and swarmed around James, Culpa, and Roget.

Kiljoy shrank back into the safety of Roget's pocket, saying, "I knew this would happen!"

A net of thorny brambles had been thrown over the travelers, trapping them. Every move resulted in a prickly poke.

The little men surrounded James and company. They wore loincloths around their scrawny waists and leveled thorny little spears at their captives.

"Don't move or it'll be all the more painful!" shouted a little man, stepping forward to inspect his prisoners.

James, Roget, Culpa, and Kiljoy stood very still.

"This is all my fault!" cried the goat.

Kiljoy popped out of Roget's pocket, certain they were in trouble. He said with pride, "See? What did I tell you? Why doesn't anyone listen to me?"

The pale little man put his little hands on his little bony hips and paced back and forth in front of them.

"So! Now we have you," he crowed triumphantly.

"Yes, you do," said James.

"Yes, indeed, we do," repeated the little man. "That we do. Don't you doubt it."

"I don't," said James.

"We have you right where we want you!" reiterated the little man.

"Yes, of course you do!" said Roget, smiling and applauding. "Good for you! A fine job of capturing!"

The crowd of miniature warriors cheered.

"Who are you?" asked James.

"Who are *you*?" the little man countered.

"I'm James."

"What are you doing here?" he demanded.

"I'm headed to Average to become king," said James matter-of-factly.

"Oh, no!" said a voice in the crowd. "*He's* gonna be the king?!"

"Uh oh!" came another voice.

"*Now* we're gonna get it!" moaned another little man, hiding behind some others. His knees were shaking.

"What're we going to do?" quivered another.

The tribe of little pink warriors flushed a darker shade and began wringing their hands and shaking their heads, moaning and saying things like, "Now, we've done it!" and "Oh boy, are *we* in trouble!"

The leader darted his head this way and that, looking for an ambush. He raised his hands to calm the tribe. He looked again at James, Culpa, Roget, and Kiljoy in the net and edged closer. He crooked his finger at James, imploring him to bend down. James obliged.

"Is this some sort of trap?" the man asked in a whisper.

"Of course it's a trap, you ninny!" barked Kiljoy. "And *we're* in it!"

"We're not Ninnies!" shouted the leader. "We're Nellies!"

"The Ninnies live over there." A little man popped up above the other Nellies and pointed south.

"You're Nellies?" asked James.

"Ah ha! So, you've heard of us," boasted the leader.

"No," James confessed.

The chief deflated and turned, shouting to his tribe, "He hasn't heard of us!"

Another chorus ensued: "Oh, no!"

"How can that happen?"

"I thought everyone knew us!" There was a lot of tsk-tsking. Some Nellies held their chins. Others hugged themselves tightly in fear and scratched their heads nervously. They all bit their nails.

Suspiciously, the little man approached the captives.

"Why haven't you heard of us? We're the Nervous Nellies! We're known all over these parts. I'm the chief Nellie."

Kiljoy, still in a foul mood, puffed up in righteous anger. "We haven't heard of you because you're little, you're ugly, and you're stupid! And we're even stupider to be caught by the likes of you!"

"Now, now, my friend," began Roget calmly. "Do not get 'zem upset with us."

The little man slowly walked back to address his tribe. "He says we're ugly and stupid!"

James held his breath. This insult couldn't lead to anything good.

The little men got more and more agitated. They began feverishly pacing back and forth, wringing their hands, beating their chests, and beseeching the sky, imploring the gods to not strike them dead.

"We're stupid!" howled a voice. "And we're ugly, too!"

"This is terrible!!" cried several little worried warriors.

James and his companions prepared for another attack.

Several of the warriors minced forward. As they did, tiny bumps started protruding from their skin. When the bumps reached the size of peas, the men pulled them off and threw them at their captives.

One landed on Kiljoy and stuck to him.

"Ow! Oh, no!" Kiljoy cried. "Worry warts! Get them off me!" He shrank down into Roget's pocket for safety.

The little warriors began hurling more worry warts. Some landed on James. They were very sticky and stung like a hundred pinpricks once attached, and hurt even worse when pulled off.

The group writhed and ducked in the net of thorns, getting pelted and pricked. Roget maneuvered in front to take the brunt. "Do not worry, my friends. Sticks and stones—"

"Will break your bones and seriously hurt!" interjected Kiljoy as he pulled another worry wart off his nose. "Ow!" Meanwhile, the tiny prickly bombs bounced off the optimist like so much confetti.

"Do not worry, *mon ami!*" said Roget. "Go on! Do your worst! I am rubber and you are glue! What bounces off me sticks to you!"

"It's not working!" shouted the chief. "Oh, no!" His knees knocked as he retreated back into the crowd of Nellies.

James heard several shouts: "This is too much!"

"It's no use!"

"I can't take this anymore!"

"What can we do?"

"Let's get outta here!!" shouted another Nellie.

"RUUUUNNNN!" they all hollered.

They ran to and fro, randomly bumping into each other as they tried to escape. Several climbed over each other in their rush to hide in the thorny thicket. The thicket trembled as it filled with Nellies.

James laughed. This was definitely the funniest thing he'd ever seen.

For the Nellies, that was the last straw. Someone shouted, "They're not afraid! Run for your lives!" They scattered, shrieking in every direction.

"Wow!" was all James could muster. "I really thought we were in trouble there."

"We *were* in trouble. And I told you so," said Kiljoy, leaning out from his perch, pulling off the last worry wart stuck to the top of his head. "Ow! If you'd only listened to me..."

"Everything came out fine! 'Zere was nothing to worry for," Roget countered and cast a sharp gaze down at the puny pessimist. "You are just what you should be: a nagging little voice 'zat does not bother us in 'ze least."

"Oh, what's the use?" The little pessimist threw up his hands and dove back down in Roget's pocket.

Culpa grabbed the thorny net in his teeth and bit a big hole in it. They all climbed out.

"Nellies are mean but they'll believe anything they're told," Culpa explained. "I should have told them right away we would destroy them if they didn't let us go. It's all my fault! I've made us even later. First the river and now Nellies! Not goo-ood." He started casting about for something to ram.

Not wanting to waste any more time, James said, "I have an idea."

"What's that?" asked the goat.

"Giddyap! I mean, let's go!"

CHAPTER 7

Average

LEAVING THE NERVOUS Nellies behind, James and company rounded one final hill to see Median City up close at last. Culpa explained that as the capital of Average, Median City was where the next king would dwell and rule. The city was not large and magnificent with huge impressive spires and domes, as one might imagine. Neither was it tiny and disappointing. It was a normal walled city, exactly the kind one would expect to see in a land called Average. The outer wall had a large gate flanked by two round stone towers. James could see the tops of several houses poking up above the wall. Toward the middle was the main castle, a collection of square buildings built of stone, connected in a way that made it clear that very little planning had gone into it.

They stood before the tall, heavy gate. James dropped his head back to see if this castle gate came down like a drawbridge, in which case they would be crushed, and he was relieved to find large hinges on either side of the gate, making it swing out like barn doors. On a parapet above the door, he thought he saw the heads of a few people quickly duck out of sight.

Culpa hollered, "He's heee-ee-rrre!"

The gate swung open to reveal a large, imposing man waiting impatiently with his arms crossed. Beefy and tall, he looked down at James and his entourage with a serious expression. His frizzy black moustache covered his upper lip like a hairy caterpillar, connected to bushy sideburns from cheek to jaw.

"Welcome to Median City. I'm the gatekeeper. We expected you sooner." He was dressed in a heavy gray coat that came to his knees. It was double breasted with dull brass buttons. It might have been an impressive uniform but for the fact it had no military insignias, braids, ribbons, or medals. *Maybe this is the uniform of Average,* James thought.

The gatekeeper was the first formidable-looking grown-up James had encountered since entering the Realm of Possibility. It made him nervous. "You've been expecting me?" asked James, not knowing what to say or what to do with his hands.

"That's right, a *little birdie* told me you were coming." James didn't much appreciate the gatekeeper's tone. It sounded condescending, as if he were speaking to a little child.

Then the gatekeeper clapped and rubbed his hands together in anticipation. "You're here now, that's what matters. Follow me! We've got some things to do before your test." He strode briskly up the cobbled street and rounded the corner.

James felt ill. It was the same sick feeling he always got in his stomach before a test. "Do I have to?"

"As I said, we must see just how average you really are," Culpa said.

"But—," began James.

"No time to lose. Come alo-ong."

"Where to?" asked James.

"The House of Commons, of course!" said the goat over

his shoulder, already clopping down a narrow street after the gatekeeper. James and Roget hurried to catch up.

You can't do anything, can you? Can you? Can you?!! echoed loudly in James's head.

"I-I'm not very good at tests," James mumbled.

"That's good to know," said the goat.

"No need to worry!" said Roget. "After all, 'ow hard can it be?"

"I'd cheat if I were you!" Kiljoy said.

"Is that allowed?" James asked.

"Depends," said the gatekeeper as they rounded the corner. He was waiting for them in front of an ornate double doorway.

"Depends on what?"

"On what an average person would do in a similar situation," the gatekeeper replied dryly. "I'll be keeping my eye on you. But, of course, the judges have the final word."

James felt terribly uncomfortable and squirmed inside knowing he was being singled out and looked at.

Beads of sweat sprang to his forehead and one trickled down the back of his ear. He feared the gatekeeper would see him for the ill-equipped, inept coward he was and report it.

"What are the judges like?" James asked anxiously. "Are they mean? Strict? Or—"

"Too many questions!" Culpa whispered. "That won't do. Don't forget, curiosity killed the cat!" he warned. "You don't want to be a *murderer*, do you?"

James gulped. He felt completely unprepared for whatever came next. "I suppose not."

"Of course not! Of course, I'd have to take the blame for it," nodded the goat. "Not that I'd mind."

"Er, did curiosity really kill 'ze cat?" ventured Roget to the gatekeeper.

"Do you see any cats?" he replied.

James worried aloud, "Can't you just *see* how average I am?" The butterflies in his stomach were zooming around like jet planes.

"Follow me," said the gatekeeper, leading them through town in procession.

The Average folk watched from their houses as the group walked down the street. The gatekeeper said to James out the side of his mouth, "Watch your step, now. Try to look and act like an average king."

Is this the test? James fretted. Not knowing who else might be watching him and judging him—and on what?—James tried to act king-like. But the more he thought about it, the more awkward and self-conscious he became.

James snuck a peek at some of the nondescript people observing him from their windows and doorways. *They must be Average citizens,* James thought. *What do they think of their prospective king?* He tried smiling and waving to them regally as he had once seen a prince do in a parade on television. From the corner of his eye, he stole a few glances at the people lining the street. Each person looked pretty much like the next and he didn't want to stare, so he kept face-forward and let everyone gawk at him. His embarrassment slowly turned into panic. Nevertheless, he pasted on as genuine a smile as he could muster. With a few quick extra steps and some shifting from left to right, James fell in rhythm with the others, matching his steps to theirs.

With every step, he felt worse and sweated more. Was this part of the test? Was he being led to the test? Was he being too clever? Was he too dense to understand anything?

By the time they reached the stone steps of a very imposing stone building, James was trembling. His tongue felt like it was wrapped in cotton.

The gatekeeper opened the door and motioned for James to enter. He did, followed by Culpa, Roget, and Kiljoy. They now stood in a great open hall. Grand portraits hung on the walls.

"This way," said the gatekeeper.

James dutifully followed as the gatekeeper led the way down a zigzag corridor. Roget shouldered his cane like a rifle. Culpa clopped loudly alongside them. No one spoke. James's heart climbed up farther and farther into his throat.

"Here we are," said Culpa, stopping in front of an imposing carved wooden door with a plaque on it that read "Common Room."

"Look," said James, finally finding his voice. "This was a bad idea. I'm going to disappoint everyone."

His tongue stuck to the roof of his parched mouth. "I-I have no idea how to take this test of yours. What I was thinking? Let's forget the whole thing. I want to go home. I-I can't do this."

Culpa and the gatekeeper exchanged shocked and disappointed looks.

"You give up?" asked the gatekeeper. "Just like that?"

James nodded as one small teardrop dribbled from his brimming eyes.

"It's all right, James. It's my fault," said Culpa, sincerely saddened. "I brought you here. My mistake! Not yours."

The lump in his throat made it impossible for James to speak. He stood there, knowing they saw what a terrible person he was. His heart hammered in his chest and he felt sick to his stomach knowing everyone saw what he was: a lousy quitter. A good-for-nothing, foolish, presumptuous little boy.

The gatekeeper marched down the hall, pointing to a smaller door and said, "Stay in there while I give the council the bad news."

James's eyes stung. He stared at the floor, utterly ashamed. He couldn't look Culpa in the face. He shrugged apologetically, blinking back tears, and trudged into the chamber.

CHAPTER 8

Home

JAMES TURNED TO SURVEY the room and got a shock. He wasn't in a castle chamber; he was in his own bedroom!

He shot a look out the bedroom door, hoping to catch a glimpse of the little scapegoat trotting down the castle hall with the gatekeeper, but all he saw was the familiar hallway with its dirty white shag carpet and the bathroom across the hall. He really was home. How could this happen?!

Then he heard his mom clomping up the stairs.

James quickly shut the door and locked it.

James was mystified. No, stupefied! He glanced at his alarm clock next to the plastic model of the biplane he made last summer. It was seven o'clock. Had all this happened to him since this afternoon? There were his stacks of comic books on his nightstand where they always were.

Had he passed through some parallel universe? Or had he just been living the most vivid daydream in history?

Whatever it was, James had to deal with the fact that he was no longer in the Realm of Possibility. He wondered if he should tell anyone about this. *No,* he thought. *Who would I tell?* It was unbelievable. His mother would think he was losing his mind.

Maybe she could finally get rid of me and be free. Being insane won't be so bad. He didn't feel at all bad about hallucinating

Mayor Culpa, Monsieur Roget, and even the grumpy Kiljoy. He'd enjoyed their wild adventures at the River Maunder and with the Nervous Nellies.

Maybe being insane is the best thing to be.

How can you live with yourself when you know you make everyone you love so miserable? James loved his mother despite everything. It hurt knowing she didn't love him. But he didn't hate her. Who else did he have? No one, that's who. Life might not even be worth living with no one to love.

He was in the midst of one of his rare dark moods; this one was serious and could last for days. James didn't care. He looked in the mirror and saw a stupid, worthless, good-for-nothing boy. He grabbed the nearest comic book and hurled it at his reflection, then he threw himself onto the bed. Immediately, he jumped back in shock. This sent his model airplane, radio, and everything else on his nightstand crashing to the floor. There, sprawled on the bed, luxuriating in the softness of the covers, lay Roget, hands behind his head, smiling up at him. Kiljoy peeked out warily from his pocket.

"'Allo!" he said. "Nice place, *mon ami.*"

"Then, it wasn't a dream?" James exclaimed.

"Obviously!" Kiljoy said with a roll of his eyes.

There was a knock on the door. His mom! She rattled the locked doorknob. "James, what are you doing in there?"

Roget was about to speak, but before he could, James's hand quickly covered his mouth. With his other hand, James stuffed the tiny pessimist deep into Roget's pocket. "Shhhh!"

James pushed Roget into the closet and tried to close the door, but it wouldn't close all the way. The pile of clothes on the floor was too big. James threw some of the rumpled shirts over Roget, burying him in the pile.

He heard another rattle of the doorknob and an impatient knock. James stood stock still, holding his breath.

Then he heard his mother mutter something he couldn't make out before she gave up and went into her room. When James heard her door shut, he breathed a sigh of relief.

He pressed his back against the door. What should he do with Roget and Kiljoy? His mom would completely freak out if she saw them. He carefully unlocked and opened his door and stole down the hall to listen at his mother's bedroom door.

She was on the phone again with Sadie.

"Sadie?" A pause and then she continued. "No, he's in his room making noise. You're so lucky your Irving is grown and out of the house. What am I going to do with him? All the time he hangs around the house making my life miserable. Now I'm supposed to leave work early to talk to his stupid teacher. How should I know if he studies? What good would it do if he did? He's just like his father. Dumb as a post and good for nothing. I tell you, he's ruining my life!"

James snuck back to his room, but the optimist and his little pet were not where he left them. His stomach flip-flopped.

"Monsieur Roget?" whispered James.

No response.

"Hey! Are you still here?"

No answer.

"That's it," he declared. "I have officially lost my mind." He heaved a huge sigh, trying to make room in his chest for an aching heart.

"It was a stupid idea anyway. Me, the King of Average? I was out of my mind." James let out another big sigh. Depression settled around him like a warm, comfy blanket.

He turned to climb into bed, but stopped when he saw a large lump under the covers. The lump gently rose up and down. Someone was breathing under there.

CHAPTER 9

A Reversal of Fortune

"**MONSIEUR ROGET!**" James shouted as he pulled back the covers.

"Don't touch me!" shrieked a loud, unpleasant voice. "What if I were dreaming of dying? When you wake a dreamer in the middle of dream it can *kill* him!"

There sat Kiljoy, life-sized and dressed in Roget's suit and vest. The clothes hung off his skinny frame, making him look like a weirdly dressed stick figure. His bulbous nose wiggled and his scowl was pinched and grim.

"What's happened to you?" James exclaimed. "You're so…"

"So what? Big? I have to be in emergencies like this. I thrive on catastrophe! I hate it when this happens, but I should have expected it!"

James was astonished to see the agitated, life-sized pessimist in optimist's clothing pacing back and forth, shaking his head.

"Where's Roget?" James shouted.

"Where should he be at a time like this? In here!" Kiljoy patted the vest pocket, now buttoned shut.

"Ow! It is okay. I am alright." Came a familiar, muffled voice. James saw a little round bulge wiggling and writhing. "It's okay! I am 'ere! Not to worry!" squeaked the tiny French voice. "Everything is fine…."

"What have you done to him?" growled James.

"Me? Ha! *I* didn't do a thing. *You* were the one who lost hope! This idiot in here…," —Kiljoy patted the pocket—"lives on hope—literally!"

"Ow! It's okay. I am all right!"

"He can die from your hopelessness! It's contagious! And where would that leave me?" Kiljoy's voice rose as he ranted on. "At least when he's small like this he can live on the barest chance, the tiniest shred of hope, but for how long? Who knows! We've got no business being here and I have no talent for getting us out of this mess." He glowered at James contemptuously.

"Poor me! Why even try? Wah, waa waa!" Kiljoy mocked. "Hmmph!"

"I'm sorry!"

"Oh, *you're* sorry?" Sneered Kiljoy. "No scapegoat to put it on this time?"

James didn't know what to say.

"Quitter! I *knew* this would happen! What good are you? You, you… good-for-nothing little worm."

"Don't say that!" he exploded. "I am so GOOD FOR SOMETHING!"

"What did you say?" Kiljoy asked defensively. "You're *what?*"

"I'm good enough for the likes of you! You… you naysayer! All right, maybe I'm not much, but I can be average! I could've been the King of Average! You, you… you… pessimist!" James spat.

"That does it," said Kiljoy indignantly. "I'm outta here!"

Kiljoy looked around for an exit and charged into the closet, kicking the clothes out of his way and slamming the door shut. James heard his muffled complaints through the door. "There we were, minding our own business! And then he comes along, and you get all het up for adventure."

James hurried over to the closet. "That's not the way out!" he said, yanking open the door. "That's the clos—"

The stone hallway of the castle lay before him. James snapped his head around; his room was gone. He was back in the Realm of Possibility; he was shocked, thrilled and relieved all at the same time.

He dashed around the corner to look for Kiljoy, the gatekeeper or Culpa. But the hallway was empty. He looked back to see once more where he had come from and his heart leapt.

There was Roget, big as life, the same dapper optimist once again, monocle firmly planted between his smiling cheek and twinkling eye. James threw his arms around him, overjoyed. Then, casting his eyes down, he saw a familiar bulge in Roget's vest pocket.

Roget smiled with a wink.

"How did you...? How does Kiljoy...? When did you two...? Why does he...?" A hundred questions burbled out of his mouth.

"Ah, again with 'ze questions!" Roget chuckled. "Do not kill 'ze cat. I am myself again and back by your side. And that, *mon ami*, is that."

Roget dropped his arm around James's shoulder and walked him down the hallway.

"Kiljoy and I, we 'ave our ups and downs. When you put Kiljoy in his place I started feeling more like myself. *Merci*, James. Thank you."

Roget lowered his voice, leaned in closer to James, and spoke confidentially. "Do not pay too much attention to

Kiljoy when he gets like that. 'E can blow up at a moment's notice, but it never lasts. Sometimes, 'e gets everything all out of proportion. He is such an overdramatizer, *histrionique,* hysterical! Always making 'ze mountain from 'ze anthill. As for *moi?* If it looks bleak, and it is difficult to see 'ze good, I feel very small. Not often! I am a professional! But no matter 'ow bad it gets, there is always something good if you try. You must believe me."

James was so relieved to have the fully restored optimist back to normal size, he simply smiled and didn't question it further.

"We'd better find Mayor Culpa and get on with the test, or whatever it is. After all, what's the worst that can happen?" said James, knowing the worst had already happened and he had survived; no, prevailed.

Kiljoy rose out of his pocket to say something but Roget immediately pushed him back down. "Mmmnnnnffff!"

"Oui."

CHAPTER 10

The Laws of Average

THE GATEKEEPER LED everyone back to the Common Room in the House of Commons where the laws of Average are made. Culpa was already there pleading his case.

"My fault! Not his!" said the scapegoat. "He's not to blame. I beg of you!" He lowered his head and began to butt it against the wall.

Eight judges sat on either side of a long wooden table: four men on one side and four women on the other. They wore identical judge's robes. Each had a notebook and an old-fashioned adding machine in front of them. The men wore white powdered wigs. The women's hair was coifed in similar fashion. Their expressions ranged from benign amusement to downright anger.

"What is the meaning of this?" objected the first presiding judge. He sat tall in his seat, like a general on a horse. He had a thick white handlebar moustache that matched the powdery white of his wig. "You are late!"

"*Unusually* late!" added the woman across the table from him. She sat straight in her chair, pursing her lips while tapping out calculations on her adding machine and noting them in her ledger.

"*Atypical*," cited a third judge, a gaunt and grim- looking lady with soft, pouchy bags under her eyes. She barely looked up while scribbling notes and doing very complex computations on her adding machine.

"That's *un*expected. Not at all what we had in mind," said another judge seated across from her. He was slightly chubby with beefy cheeks and big bags under his half-lidded eyes.

"We were expecting... something else," said the fourth woman judge, looking very much like her male counterpart. She leafed through a large book.

"Although," she said, "this has happened from time to time." She flipped back a few pages and quoted, "Tardiness can occur once in ten years and three times in a hundred." She addressed the other judges with arms outspread. "According to the Law of Averages, it was *bound* to happen."

A sixth judge typed madly on his adding machine. A length of adding-machine paper rolled out in a long ribbon across the desk. "According to my calculations it is within reason, but just barely."

"Agreed," said the seventh and eighth judges. They were a younger couple. Both had round, cheerful faces and when they realized they had spoken simultaneously, they hooked pinkies and said, "Bread and butter!"

"Ahem!" said the first judge. The young pair immediately sat up and tried to look grave.

"Still, it is unusual. Not good," maintained the first man grudgingly.

James stepped forward. "I'm sorry if I wasted anyone's time."

"Don't listen to him! Comple-eeee-tly my fau-auult, your honor! I throw myself on the mercy of the court." The scapegoat leapt onto the table, bleating madly in the judges' faces, then bounded off and crashed into the wall with his hard head of horns.

The judges stood up and applauded. "Bravo!"

"Order! Order!" demanded the first judge. The room fell silent. "Apology accepted."

Culpa nuzzled James's arm affectionately. James patted the silly goat, and Roget patted James on the shoulder in much the same manner.

"Now, down to business," said the Chief Judge, planting his hands on the desk and standing up. He leaned toward them. "Young man, we're here to determine your suitability to reign as king of all, or at least most, of Average."

"Oh, 'e will be a magnificent king!" said Roget, bowing respectfully.

"Who are you?" demanded the judge.

"Monsieur William Roget, Optimist. A fellow traveler and recent acquaintance of Monsieur James."

"We don't want or need a *great* king," the judge said. "We need an *average* king!"

"Oh, I'm sure 'e can be that, too...." Roget trailed off, fearing he may have ruined James's chances.

"Who exactly are you?" James countered. The judge raised his eyebrows. "To be so rude to... my... er, um..." James tried to finish his thought.

"We are not *exactly* anybody!" The judge banged his gavel and settled into his chair. "We regulate Average from this House of Commons. We maintain standards for Average and make the law for our commonwealth."

He grabbed his lapels and stood proudly. "We are charged with maintaining the status quo."

"Keeping things on par," avowed the second judge.

"Balancing the budget," added the third woman with the thin lips.

"Moderating the usual things," the fourth judge added.

"Regulating the regular things," stated the fifth.

"Making sure things are fair-to-middling," affirmed the sixth.

"Passable," said the seventh judge.

"Sort of," the eighth added.

"In other words," said the first, "we formulate the Law of Average."

"I see," said James. "Then why do you need a king? It looks like you're the ones in charge."

"Bite your tongue!" the Chief Judge barked.

"Every kingdom needs a king," said the second judge, rising to her feet. "If we didn't, we would be…"

"Unusual," said the third, rising to her feet.

"Remarkable," added the fourth.

"Extraordinary, when we must be... ordinary," said the fifth.

"Ridiculous!" said the sixth.

"We must have a king!" judges seven and eight chimed in.

The first judge banged his gavel. "Enough! Be seated!" He turned his attention to James.

"We are a mediocracy, and as such we *must* have a king. That's the way things are and shall always be. We can't change it."

"It's just not done!" said the second judge.

"Can't have that, I guess," said James. "Well then, I'm your man!"

"Are you, really?" scoffed the first man. His eyes narrowed, scrutinizing James carefully.

James flushed and faltered, embarrassed at his own boast that had slipped out without thinking. "Well, no! Of course not! I mean, I could be—if you think I should be. But I'm pretty sure I could be really, er, totally average if I really, really tried... I guess..." His cheeks flushed.

"I mean, I know I'm nothing special or anything but... but..." James stammered. His palms began to sweat. "I'd like to at least give it a try?" It was as much a declaration as a question. James shrugged and stared at the floor.

The eight judges hurried into a huddle. They gabbled and feverishly gesticulated, and then, just as quickly, sat back down.

"You seem a likely candidate," said the first man.

James exhaled. "I passed? I'm king?"

He smiled and turned to his friends. "That wasn't as bad as I thought."

"Not so fast," the Chief Judge said. "Let us tell you about your quest."

CHAPTER 11

The Quest

"QUEST?! WHAT QUEST?! Who said anything about a quest?!" shouted Kiljoy.

"Every king must quest for a crown! It's the law! And more than that, it's *expected*," said the Chief Judge.

The seventh judge added, "A King of Average must be what everyone expects." She smiled and batted her eyes.

"You can be or do nothing out of the ordinary," said the eighth.

"Once you are king it is forbidden to violate this rule. That constitutes failure and you will be banished," said the first judge.

"You must accept things as they are and live within your limitations. If you meet all—or most of—our expectations, then all is well. Exceed them and be banished to the lands above Average. Fail and you will be disgraced and banished to the lands below."

"But what if—?" James began.

"Enough! If you need all the answers now, then there's no reason to consider you any further," said the first judge. His gavel came down.

Bang!

Kiljoy quietly crept from Roget's pocket and climbed up James's sleeve to whisper, "Give up now and save us all a lot of trouble." He crept back into the optimist's pocket.

James felt queasy. The room went fuzzy.

"*Excusez-moi, mes amis!*" piped Roget. "I am absolutely sure that Monsieur James can be your king! I know '*e* may not question you, but is it permissible if I... er, we—" He indicated Kiljoy hiding in his pocket and the distraught Culpa—"'elp him on his quest?"

Again the judges huddled.

"By all means, yes. In fact, if he accomplished this all by himself, that *would* be extraordinary and disqualify him immediately," said the kindly eighth man.

"You can bring along as much help as you need, but no more," said the seventh judge very nicely. She smiled. "Everyone needs a little help now and again. It's normal," she added with a wink.

"That is, if anyone is stupid or brave enough to risk throwing in with you," warned the fourth man.

"Because if you help him and he fails, we banish the lot of you."

Kiljoy screamed and fainted into the bottom of Roget's pocket.

Culpa stepped forward and stood at attention. "If he fails, it won't be his fault."

"Well?" asked the judge.

James saw the little scapegoat standing proudly at his side. Roget twirled his moustache and struck a heroic pose while Kiljoy lay unconscious in his vest pocket. James was touched. Nobody had ever offered to help him do anything before, nor had anyone ever been so encouraging. For an instant, he felt absolutely certain. He turned to the panel and announced, "I accept!"

A cheer went up around the table.

"Very well," said the first judge. "Here is your task: You must find our former king. Discover why he renounced the mediocracy. Return and swear you'll never aspire to be any greater or less than expected and you shall be our new king."

The first judge made his way around the table, gesturing to James to come view a large map on the wall.

"This map shows the places we think our last king may have gone."

"What was his name?" James dared another question.

"Norman the Unexceptional," all eight judges intoned wistfully.

"For many years, he was so—adequate!"

"Tremendously mediocre!" They all nodded.

"So typical," the second lady judge said nostalgically. "He was *everyone's* idea of a king."

All eight judges sighed in admiration. The first judge shook himself out of his reverie and got back to business.

"We think he might have headed here, to the lands above Average."

"That means he may have done something senseless, like try to excel," said the second judge. She gestured to the map. The places surrounding Average had names like Expect Station, Envia, Uppity, Nobbling, Hearsay, Accusia, and Superior.

"Or he may have given up entirely and be somewhere down around Lake Inferior, here," the first judge said as he pointed to a blue patch on the map.

The places below Average had names like Dullsville, Appathia, Paranoia, Desperation, and Disappointment Bay.

The Sea of Doubt went off the very edge of the map. "He could be here, there, or somewhere else. We simply don't know," the seventh kind lady judge added. "We are fairly certain he is somewhere." She smiled. "That's the situation in a nutshell."

"Nicely done," the third judge allowed. "Just enough to go on."

"I don't know where to begin!" said James.

The eight judges applauded.

"Well said. Oh, you'll make a very average king! I have no doubt," said the first judge.

The rest of the judges grumbled and cleared their throats.

"I mean, I have *little* doubt," he restated. "If you return, that is."

"Ahhhhh, better," they all nodded approvingly.

The first judge took James by the shoulder and led him to the door. "Come back in a reasonable amount of time and let us know what you find out."

Then, James, Culpa, and Roget were standing in the hallway. The door slammed shut behind them.

The gatekeeper was waiting and herded them down the hall. "This way," he said.

"Can you tell me anything that would help?" James pleaded with the gatekeeper. "I don't have any idea what to do."

The gatekeeper shook his head. "You know what they say? Ignorance is bliss! Thank you for coming and have a nice day." He pushed them out and shut the gate.

CHAPTER 12

The Middle of the Road

JAMES STOOD for some time, hesitating to choose a direction. He looked up to see the judges, the gatekeeper, and a few townsfolk peering down at them from the parapet.

The road leading away from the castle stretched like a ribbon through the hills and disappeared at the horizon.

"I guess we should 'follow the yellow brick road,'" James said with a smile.

"What are you talking about?" Kiljoy called from Roget's pocket. "The road's not brick! It's dirt! I told you he's nuts," he said to Roget.

"I was making a joke," said James.

"There, you see? 'E was joking again," said Roget, still not getting it.

"Mayor Culpa, any idea which way to go?" asked James.

"You have to make a choice. They're watching to see what *you'll* do-oo, not me-ee-e," said the scapegoat. "But whatever you choose, if it's not the right way, I'm here for you. Blame me-ee-e."

"All right, then." James took a deep breath. "Follow me. We'll just stick to the middle of the road and see where it takes us."

"Hooray!" A cheer went up from the gallery above them.

Soon the city gates disappeared behind the hill. The road rolled ahead, winding around one hill and over the next. But the farther from Average they went, the less distinct the road became. Finally, it was indistinguishable from the earth and grass patches that spread out before them in all directions.

CHAPTER 13

The Shadow

JAMES WAS GLAD for the long walk; it gave him time to reflect on his experience in the Realm of Possibility. So much had happened in such a short time. He still hadn't a clue how he had gotten here. Could the Shubins' yard be a portal? Or was it because he had said out loud thoughts best kept to himself? Did giving voice to your innermost desires make things happen? If so, he'd consider saying a lot more things. Did things like this happen to everybody? *Why me and why now? And what about—?* James stopped mid-thought. *Better not even think too many questions. Why ruin my chances?*

"What happened to the road?" asked James, snapping out of his reverie.

"Isn't it obvious?" Kiljoy whined. "You've gotten us hopelessly lost."

"Lost, *oui!*" said Roget. "But not 'opelessly. Right, your demi-'ighness?"

"Demi-highness?" asked James.

"You are not yet king, but I think you should get used to being treated as one. You are not yet a "ighness' as I would call a king. But I think you are something...admirable. You are almost a king so I will call you your demi-'ighness. It means 'alf a king."

"You don't have to call me anything," said James, feeling the heat of a blush in his face.

"Ah, *non, mon ami*. A demi-king deserves respect." Roget bowed deeply. "I am your loyal servant."

"We're still lost no matter what you call him," Kiljoy reminded him.

"My mind wandered, I guess," James said apologetically.

"You guess?! It's perfectly obvious," said Kiljoy.

"Lost in thought, eh?" mused Roget. "Ah, well. Perhaps it will lead us to more adventure," he said, beaming with his trademark enthusiasm. "One never knows. That is 'ze fun, *oui*?"

"No!" countered Kiljoy. "That is the danger!"

"I'm sorry," James said, reflexively expecting a reprimand from Culpa, but it didn't come. A quick look around revealed the little scapegoat was gone.

"Mayor Culpa?" James called. How could he have wandered off so quickly? There was nowhere to hide. "Monsieur Roget, did you see where Mayor Culpa...?"

But now Roget and Kiljoy were gone too! James was alone, standing in the middle of—well, the middle of nowhere.

"Monsieur Roget? Kiljoy? *Anybody?!*"

The sun was going down, touching the top of the hills in the distance. Soon it would be dark. What was happening? Nothing looked familiar. It was eerily similar to the first time he had stumbled into the Realm of Possibility. In the blink of an eye everything was different. This was new territory.

"Where am I?"

"You're neither here, nor there, James," whispered an ominous voice. James looked down and saw a long, gangly shadow on the ground creeping toward him. His knees wobbled and cold dread churned his stomach. "Won't you say hello to an old friend?"

"Do I know you?" James asked, after a hard, dry swallow.

"Intimately," it replied. "And what do you think you're doing?"

"I'm on a quest," James answered, "to become the King of—"

"Of nothing!" it snarled.

James's insides froze. The Shadow crept closer, becoming one with his shadow, made larger and longer with the setting sun. James gasped.

"Don't worry. There's no need to be afraid of me. You know me, don't you?"

Despite the reassurance, fear froze him for an instant. Then through his terror, James managed to say, "I-I'm sorry, I don't."

"Oh, come now," it prodded. "I know we don't talk much, but you must recognize me."

"No. I-I don't. I'm sorry. I've got to go now."

The Shadow chuckled. "Oh, I don't think so. We're going to stay right here, you and I," it said, "and get reacquainted."

"I really can't."

"Now, now. None of that, James. It won't do."

"But my friends..."

"What friends?!" it scoffed. "Look around. They're all gone. And I'll tell you why. You didn't fool them. They finally saw you for what you are! A nothing, a nobody! Not worth the time of day. Look here."

The Shadow began to morph from the shape of a little boy into a figure so ugly and horrifying James couldn't look.

"Don't turn away!"

"No!" James shut his eyes tight. If what the Shadow showed him were true he'd rather die than exist as such a hideous thing.

Suddenly a loud flapping and fluttering of wings rushed overhead. A little blackbird with orange-tipped wings dove at him and whizzed past: it was the same bird who'd attacked him just before he'd first entered the Realm of Possibility.

"Wraawwk!" It darted away.

James sprang forward, detaching from the writhing shape. He ran as fast as he could after the bird. The faster he ran, the more distance he made from himself and the monstrous shadow. The bird sped away into the blue of the sky, growing smaller and smaller until it was a tiny dot, then gone.

When the dot vanished so did the Shadow.

James shivered from head to toe. He scanned the horizon, staring into the blinding rays of the setting sun. A familiar voice called out, "'Allo?! Ahh! There you are!"

Roget and Culpa stood silhouetted against the remaining sun.

"Baa-aa-aah! Where did you go?! I thought we'd lost you!" the goat bleated. "It's all my fault, James! I'm sor-rr-yy!"

James ran to them and locked them into a tight embrace.

"Oof! Thank you my demi-'ighness," said Roget. "Strange, I left your side but for a minute, then poof! You were gone. But I found our friend, 'ze mayor. I followed 'is tracks a short way and there 'e was! Clever of me, *non?*"

"Dumb luck!" said Kiljoy.

"Where *did* you go?" Roget asked.

James looked down at his feet. There was no sign of the Shadow.

"I was *nowhere*. And now I'm here!" said James with a big smile and a forced laugh, hoping a little humor would erase the memory of the Shadow. "I was neither here nor there," he said. "But don't worry, I'm back now."

Roget laughed. "What? Me, worry? Never!"

"What a terrible thing I did!" wailed Culpa. "I could just kick myself! Better yet, you kick me, James. Go ahead, I deserve it." The goat presented his backside to James.

"It's all right, Mayor," said James. "I'm just glad to see you."

"Such a nice boy!" said Roget to Kiljoy, who watched this syrupy reunion with disdain. James smiled at the optimist and couldn't resist giving Roget another quick hug.

"Watch it!" cried Kiljoy. "You're crowding me!"

"Let's get out of here," said James, linking arms with Roget and grabbing Culpa by the horn. They marched toward the horizon into the last gleaming rays of daylight.

CHAPTER 14

The Ninnies and Their Fabulous King

WITH A BARELY VISIBLE path before them, James and company pressed on as the sky turned to blue, then purple. Night was upon them.

"It's no use. We're wandering around like a bunch of ninnies," groused Kiljoy.

"Ho, there! Did someone say Ninnies?" A voice came across the field.

James and Roget turned to see a small tribe of little men very much like the Nervous Nellies. They even wore similar loincloths but their skin was pale lavender, their loincloths blue. James counted a dozen. The tiny pale men advanced toward them, marching two abreast. Their movements were slow and methodical. They wore dull expressions on their faces; mouths slack-jawed, their eyes round and vacant. They stared in awe, stupefied at everything around them.

Kiljoy emerged from Roget's pocket. "They don't look too bright, do they?"

A second phalanx brought up the rear, carrying a sedan chair painted blue with gold stars haphazardly emblazoned on the sides. Inside was a man wearing a white cape trimmed with gold braid. He wore a very intricately woven straw cowboy hat with red trim around the brim and a peacock feather poking out of it. He was the same size as the other men but didn't share their dull expression. On the contrary: he was lordly, smiling and alert.

He hopped out and strutted up to James, Culpa, and Roget. Looking them up and down, he declared, "You're not Ninnies."

"No, we're not," said James.

"I heard someone say you were! I'm sure of it." The man scrutinized them suspiciously. "Are you sure you're not Ninnies?"

Kiljoy had enough. "Of course we're not ninnies, you Ninny!"

"No offense. It is a manner of speech," said Roget. "Forgive 'im."

"Because if you *were* ninnies, I'd be your master and you would be sworn to obey me, for I am King of the Ninnies." He drew himself up to his full height (which came to James's knee). "Right, everybody?" he called.

"*Right!*" they called back.

"I am Alastair the Vainglorious!" he announced resoundingly.

The crowd cheered as if on cue. "All hail the king!" They began a monotonous chant, "All hail the king! All hail the king! All hail the king! All hail—"

"That's quite enough!" Alistair cut them off with a gesture. Obediently, they stopped mid-chant. "Don't mind them. They're Ninnies," he said.

"Ah, another king! *Merveilleux!*" said Roget. "My friend James 'ere is soon to be a king 'imself."

"Is that so?" said Alistair with a cocked eyebrow.

"*Oui!*" said Roget.

"*Oui.* Er, yes," said James, "I am. My name is James and this is Mayor Culpa and Monsieur Roget and that's Kiljoy." He indicated toward the squirming bulge in the optimist's pocket.

"You're not my enemies, are you?" said Alistair warily. "Because I've led my army of Ninnies to victory in every major war against great odds and you wouldn't stand a chance!" He tilted his chin into the air.

"We're not your enemies," said James. "I'm on a quest to become King of Average."

"King of Average, eh?" said Alistair, stroking his chin, satisfied. He put his hands on his hips and puffed out his chest and boasted, "That's nothing. Me? I'm sovereign ruler of every territory there is around here except for Average." King Alistair turned to his followers. "Isn't that right?"

"Whatever you say!" the Ninnies rejoined.

"See that?" he said gallantly, placing his fists on his waist.

Kiljoy popped up to glare at the little man. "You? A general, a fighter, and the king of everywhere else? I find that hard to believe."

Alistair's smile dropped. His eyebrows knotted with worry and his lip quivered.

"It's true, I'm the greatest king *ever!*" he said. "I've done practically anything you can think of! Look! I even made this hat!"

He showed them his hat, which to James was obviously machine made and store bought.

"I made it all by myself. And… And I spun this cloth to make this cape. You name it and I've probably done it! Isn't that right, my Ninnies?"

The Ninnies all reassured Kiljoy that King Alistair was the nicest, bravest, most resourceful king they'd ever known and that he was greatest king who had ever lived.

Kiljoy responded, "What do they know? They're *Ninnies!*"

Alistair frowned and bit his lip. "It's all true… Every word."

"It's all right. You don't have to make things up to impress us," said James.

"I don't? Er, I mean, I *don't!* I'm *not!*" the king said.

"But, be honest. You'd like me a lot more if I *was* the greatest king who had ever lived, right?"

"Not really," said James.

"What? You mean, you'd like me even if—?" He lowered his voice to barely a whisper. "If I wasn't a king?"

"Sure," said James.

Alistair was astonished. "*Why?*"

"I'd like you just because."

"Just because?" Alistair thought for a moment. "Impossible! Nobody likes anybody *just because*. You have to impress everyone and make them think you do great things! Things to be admired! *'Just because'?*" he scoffed. "That's ridiculous."

"No, it's not," James insisted.

"Shhh!" said King Alistair. "Don't tell my Ninnies," he pleaded. "If they found out I—er, ah wasn't… That I didn't…

And I couldn't... They'd hate me. Or worse! They wouldn't let me be their king anymore. Promise you won't say anything!" The little man was frantic. "I'll give you anything, anything! Only please, please say you won't tell! Please, don't tell!"

This poor man, thought James.

Kiljoy popped up. "I for one would like you better if you got us out of here and told us where we can find the old King of Average. I want to get this ridiculous quest over with."

Alistair's eyes lit up. "Done!" He clapped his hands. "Ninnies! My chair! Prepare to march on the double!"

The Ninnies sprang into action. They brought out another litter and scooped James, Culpa, and Roget into it in front of Alistair's sedan chair and marched through the night, huffing and puffing. The rhythmic swaying of the chair on the shoulders of the Ninnies lulled them to sleep. At dawn, Alistair and the Ninnies deposited the group back on the middle-of-the-road, refreshed and ready for the day.

"Follow the road south to an old resort called Disappointment Bay."

"Do you know for sure he's there?" asked James.

"He has to be there," Alistair predicted. "It's the last resort." He grabbed hold of James's shirt and pulled him down and whispered, "Remember—you promised!"

Alistair hopped onto his chair and called, "Ninnies! Away!"

Alistair the Vainglorious, King of the Ninnies, waved goodbye, looking every tiny inch a departing hero. James pitied him, and resolved never to reveal the little man's terrible secret.

CHAPTER 15

Lake Inferior

JAMES, CULPA, AND ROGET followed the middle-of-the-road farther south all morning. By noon they came to a broken-down sign drooping nearly down to the ground. It read "Lake Inferior."

A few ramshackle shanties formed a village, if you could even call it that. They lined a short potholed street. The buildings faced a stagnant lake that was more like a large marshy pond. Mosquitos buzzed lazily in the air, too exhausted to bite.

"Where is everybody?" Kiljoy wondered aloud.

The four travelers headed toward the only official-looking building in town. The faded letters above the door read "Inferior Town Hall and General Store." The lettering on the filthy glass of the door read "Useless P. Malingerer, Proprietor, Deputy Mayor, Injustice of the Peace, and Magistrate of the Inferior Court."

"Anyone here?" called James.

The door was ajar. With one knock it swung open, revealing a man with a long white beard dressed in a dusty black frock coat. He bent over a loose floorboard, hastily stuffing a cloth bundle into the space below.

"Hello?" said James.

The man jumped and spun around. He put the board back, kicked a rug over it, and ran to the door.

"You can't barge in like this! What are you doing here?"

"What are *you* doing?" James asked.

"Hiding my shame! Did you see that? Oh, dear, now I'll have to find another place to hide it. Go away! Leave me alone."

"We're looking for somebody. Is there a King Norman here?" asked James.

"I couldn't say. I haven't been outside in years. None of us have."

"We're from Average," James began. "And we have to—"

"Average! You're in the wrong place. Go away. Leave us to our misery; that's all any of us deserve."

"We're looking for—" James began.

"What was it? Were you singled out? Did those boring, banal buffoons with their calculations banish you? Hmph! Those not-so-superior court judges with their calculations!" he said bitterly. "Well, if they sent you here, go find a hole to crawl into. Otherwise, leave immediately!"

"Would you please listen?" asked James. "We came to find the old King of Average."

"Do you mean Nor—" he started to say, but thought better of it. "Nope. Sorry. Nobody like that lives here. None of my business, anyway." He hastily made for the door and ushered them out. "Go away! I've got my own troubles."

"If you know anything, please tell us. It's very important that we find him."

"I can't help you."

The man tried to push them out the door, but James forced his foot between it and the doorjamb.

"Can you at least tell us the way to Disappointment Bay?"

The old man gave an exasperated sigh. "The far end of the lake, across the marsh to the Sea of Doubt. That's all I'll say." He kicked James's foot away and slammed the door shut. They heard deadbolts thrown and locks turned. The shades were swiftly drawn.

"What noo-oww?" asked Culpa.

"Give up?" Kiljoy suggested.

James had a suspicion the man had more to say. "Let's go to the far end of the lake, like he said."

They found their way to the southernmost point of Lake Inferior, which ended in a swamp. A mossy sign read "Grime Properties for Sale: Muck & Mire Realty."

They slogged through the swamp to a beach, where an abandoned pavilion built on stilts listed heavily to one side, its foundation sunk halfway into the ground.

Several small houses were also sunk in the mud. Various "For Sale" signs were planted in front of each house: "Another low-quality investment from Muck & Mire," "Unplanned Retirement Community," "Disenfranchises Available," and "Call Muck to get Stuck… with a once-in-a-lifetime opportunity!" On the front of the pavilion's weather-beaten walls, the faded sign above the entrance read "DISAPPOINTMENT BAY—THE LAST RESORT."

Past what looked to be a hotel was a beach littered with smelly kelp, driftwood, and garbage. They made their way to a single tent lit by a campfire.

Eggs and ham sizzled in a pan on the fire. It smelled amazing. The last time James had something to eat was long ago in another world. He was famished.

The shabby canvas tent was zipped up tight.

"Grab it and let's go!" whispered Kiljoy from the pocket.

"Shhhh!" hissed Roget, thumping Kiljoy on the head.

They gathered around the fire eyeing the eggs and ham; upon further inspection, the food looked slightly burnt and rubbery. Still, their mouths watered.

James spoke. "Let's ask if they'll share it with us."

"It's every man for himself," said Kiljoy.

"Go ahead. I'm not hungry anyway," a tired voice spoke from inside the tent.

"Are you sure?" asked James.

"Help yourself."

They tucked into the meal with gusto. The eggs were indeed rubbery and the ham was like leather, but they devoured every bit.

"That was, um… good. Thank you," said James, trying to get the taste out of his mouth. "We were really hungry."

"You're welcome."

An awkward silence grew more awkward the longer no one had anything to add. Roget and James exchanged glances. James thought he should at least offer their benefactor an explanation for intruding. Maybe the man could tell them the whereabouts of the former king.

"We're not from around here," said James, not quite knowing how to strike up a useful conversation. It was odd to be talking to a closed tent flap. "Would you like to know what brought us here?"

"It's quite an interesting story, *mon ami*," added Roget.

"Y'see," James continued, "I'm on a quest—"

The tent flap opened and a lanky man stepped out. He wore a blue tattered robe and a dull gold crown encrusted with unpolished gems. His long white hair was pulled back into a ponytail. He peered at the group through watery gray eyes. His sharp, prominent nose suited his face just fine.

Culpa dropped to his knees.

"Your Maa-aa-jesty!"

CHAPTER 16

Norman the Unexceptional

"**ALL RIGHT,** you found me. Now go away. Leave me alone."

James didn't move. He stared up at this statuesque, regal figure, the perfect picture of a king.

"Your ma-aa-ajesty! Whatever you did, whatever it was, it's my fault! Blame me-ee!" Culpa pleaded, prostrate at the man's feet.

"Get up. I'm nobody's king. You can't make excuses for me anymore." He strode off toward a rickety pier and untied a rowboat tethered at the far end.

"Where are you going?" James called.

"Away."

Roget gasped. "*Sacre bleu!* 'Ze Sea of Doubt! 'E will surely be lost!"

James ran after the king, grabbing his hand. It surprised them both. James held on, imploring the former king, "Don't go. Please!"

"I can't bear it anymore," the man said grimly, his eyes filled with sorrow.

"I have to know," James said. His voice cracked with emotion. "I have to know *why*. Or I can't be—"

"King. I know," Norman cut him off. "Don't bother, son. It's not worth it. Go on back and tell them I was never fit to be king in the first place. That's all they need to know."

"That's not good enough," James persisted. "Why did you leave?" Unbidden tears sprouted and leaked down his face. *Why did you leave?* It was the only question he had always wanted to ask his own father.

Norman took James by the shoulders. His forlorn gray eyes met James's. His touch was firm. James steadied himself and wiped away his tears. He felt connected somehow to the former king. It was more than sympathy, more than respect. It was kinship: a knowledge that they shared more than could ever be said in words.

Norman rose to his full height, his eyes still fastened on James's, then turned and climbed into the boat.

"Don't go. Please! Please don't go! Not like this," James begged.

"Get in."

Roget shouted from shore, "NO! Do *not* go with 'im, James! 'Ze Sea of Doubt…! You will be lost!"

"It's all over!" cried Kiljoy.

Mayor Culpa bleated for all he was worth and rushed out onto the pier. Roget followed. "If 'e goes, we *all* go!" Roget valiantly declared. Kiljoy shrieked and climbed out of Roget's pocket, ready to bail should the worst happen.

"Just you," the king said to James. "No one else."

Roget and Mayor Culpa protested, but the king reassured them he'd bring James back.

Norman looked tired as he grabbed hold of the oars and pushed away.

They rowed in silence for a while, staying in sight of the shore. Finally, he turned to James. "All right, ask."

"Why?"

"I'm not fit to be king of anything," said Norman.

The very words of the Shadow.

"No, you were a fine king!" James assured him. "Everyone said so."

"Don't tell me what I am! I'm telling you the truth!" Norman said angrily.

James paled and shrank farther back on his seat, chastened. "Yes, sir."

Norman stopped rowing and studied James. Then in a softer voice he said, "You can do much better than aspiring to the throne of Average, kid. Really."

"No. You don't understand. I-I can't," James stammered, tears welling in his eyes. Once again, he was angry at himself for the sudden emotional outburst.

"Why not?" Norman asked.

How could he explain that being average was all he could ever hope for—and even that was a risk? He wanted to prove, beyond a shadow of a doubt, to himself and to his mother, that he was not as bad as either of them thought he was. He took a deep breath and slowly exhaled, attempting to master his emotions.

"I have to try or else... or else... there's no reason I ever should have been born," he said as calmly as possible.

King Norman slowly shook his head. "So, you want to be *truly* average. The most average there ever was?"

James kept his eyes down and nodded.

"It's harder than you think."

James shrugged. "I have to try."

He reached over and touched James's shoulder and said in a voice filled with regret, "I tried, too. Tried to be a good king. To be what everybody needed me to be: adequate in all things. But in the end," he said bitterly as he swallowed hard and turned away, "I failed."

"That's not true," said James. "Everyone loved you. You were a perfectly average king. That is, until you left."

The king stared long and hard at James before casting his gaze out to sea. His voice was low and quiet. "I had a family once: a wife and kids. We were the first family of Average and I was hailed king." His eyes had a faraway look as he relived the painful memories. He exhaled heavily.

"My wife wasn't average and never wanted to be. She wanted an exceptional husband, someone rich, strong, and powerful. That wasn't me. I was just an average man. She demanded so much. She longed to be a great and powerful queen, married to a great and powerful king. She asked for more, more, and more. More of everything. No matter what I did, it was never enough. She grew to despise me. She blamed me, she blamed our children, blamed everyone but herself. She was an Accusian—beautiful, vain, and selfish."

Norman kept his eyes on the horizon. "In order to save my family, I found a scapegoat to take the blame from me, but even he couldn't handle her fury. So I gave him to my daughter and she made him her pet."

This was news to James. *Culpa was a pet?*

"Finally, my wife's contempt and hatred drove her mad. She kept herself locked in a tower, away from everyone, until one day she perished from loneliness and despair. I made excuses and decreed that no one in Average be allowed to ask too many questions. So no one did and they all believed I was happily married with a typical family. I let them believe it and remained king."

James thought of his own mother, trapped in their shabby house in a tedious job. She never went anywhere but work and home, and had nobody to talk to but her neighbor Sadie who never came over. Probably because of him. His mother was a prisoner and he was her jailer.

He hated that he made her life so miserable. There was nothing he could do but leave her alone, a prisoner in her tower. It made him sad and angry to be such a pathetic and useless son.

"That left me with just my children," Norman went on.

"Children?" James perked up.

"A boy and a girl. Twins. Just about your age."

"Where are they now?"

Norman hesitated. "Gone," he said in a choked voice. He cleared his throat. "My daughter was bright, precocious. I was so proud of her, but I was also worried I'd lose my kingdom if she was found to be above average."

"What did you do?"

Norman's eyes shone with shameful tears and he blinked them back.

"I discouraged her," he said. "I told her she wasn't half as good as she thought. I taught her to keep her talents to herself and not be proud and vain like her mother."

"Was she?" James asked.

"No! No, she was kind and sweet. But how could I have a mad wife and an exceptional daughter and still be King of Average? In the end, I secretly sent her away to a school in Superior. *For her own good,* I told myself."

He straightened up and said in a strained voice, "But I did it for me and my kingdom. I did it for my own selfish reasons."

"And your son?" asked James.

"My son?" he said ruefully. "My son was average. Just like me. Ordinary, like you want to be. He would have succeeded me. I lost him, too."

"Why? How?"

Norman slammed his fist on the rim of the boat. "Too many questions! Why do I have to explain myself to you?! He ran away! Leave it at that! He's gone for good."

Norman hung his head. "My 'happy' family was a sham. I worked so hard to *appear* average. I made everyone believe I was happy. I was hailed by all, 'King Norman the Unexceptional, good guy, hail-fellow-well- met.' But it was an act. I was a fake! A pretender to the throne of Average."

The king's face was a mask of sorrow. "I couldn't keep up the pretense. It would have come out sooner or later, so I left before anyone found out."

James didn't know what to say. Here was this strong, kind man, a victim of circumstance with a cruel wife and children he loved, confessing his failures as a man to an eleven-year-old boy.

"So, there you have it. Now you can return to Average and take my place. Become what everyone wants, what they all need: a truly average king."

They rowed back to shore.

"Don't lose yourself in the Sea of Doubt," said James as they neared the dock.

"Why not?" Norman said dolefully. "What do I have left?"

"Please..., would you stay for me?" James was surprised at his boldness but the words escaped before he could take them back. Wanting and asking for anything from his mother had always ended in anger and rejection.

Norman stared at him in disbelief. "For *you*?"

James held his breath and braced himself for the rebuff.

"You?" Norman allowed himself a smile, the first James had seen. After a moment of consideration he said, "All right, for you. For now."

James was ecstatic. He wanted to throw his arms around the man but didn't dare.

"I'll wait here to see that you take the throne before I go."

Relief, happiness, pride, and more cascaded through James all at once, feelings he'd rarely experienced. It sparked an idea.

"Your children would forgive you if they knew."

Norman's face darkened. He sat there in stony silence as the water gently lapped against the boat.

"If you told them what you told me..."

"Enough!" the former king roared with a sudden ferocity that made James shrink back in fear. The tension between them crackled electric.

When they reached the dock, James tried again.

"They have to know! They'd forgive you. I *know* they would."

"Get out!" It was a command, loud and final.

James clambered out, helped by his friends. Norman tethered the boat and climbed onto the pier.

Culpa fell to his knees once more. "My king!"

"Not anymore," said Norman. "Never again!"

The man strode off the pier and went back to his tent; he stepped inside and zipped up the flap.

"Buu-uuu-ttt, but, but... it wasn't your fault!" bleated the goat. "*I'm* to blame! Blame me! It's all my fault!! Please!" He began to butt his head violently into a boulder stuck in the sand. "Plee-ea-se... I'm to blame!!"

The tent's zipper ripped back down. Norman stepped out and stood to his full height, his eyes flashing with an anger that verged on rage.

"I AM *NOT* A KING! I AM NOBODY'S KING! Get out! Go back! Leave me be!"

James and Roget quailed and backed away. Kiljoy shrank down into Roget's pocket and pulled lint over his head.

When Norman saw how he had frightened them, his temper evaporated.

He rested a hand on James's shoulder once more. "You found me, son. Tell them what they need to hear and start your reign. Be the most average you can be. I'll be here; I've given you my word. Go and do what I couldn't. Good luck."

Norman the Unexceptional, failed King of Average, stalked off across the marsh and vanished into the hotel.

James noticed scraps of paper torn and scattered on the floor of Norman's tent and gathered them up. They were fragments of a letter.

One read:

… still won't matter to you, will we?

Another said:

… never, ever be like you… as far from Average as I can.

… never want to see you again.

Another read:

… you'll see one day… Good-bye forever.

Roget was having trouble keeping Culpa from jumping in the water. The poor goat was beside himself. He wept and bleated piteously, trying desperately to drown himself.

James stuffed the torn scraps of paper into his pocket and ran to help. When he and Roget had managed to pull the scapegoat away from the shore, Culpa ran up to one of the piers that supported the half-sunk hotel and rammed it ferociously, scarring it with several hard *thwacks* of his horns.

Eventually they were able to subdue the distraught goat and lead him away, back down the road past the shabby village and its shanties. They left Lake Inferior and its lonely inhabitants to their shame.

CHAPTER 17

Return to Average

"IT'S ALL MY FAULT!" cried the goat.

"No," James assured the goat. "He blames himself."

"Out of the question!" cried Culpa. "It is and always shall be my fault as long as I live."

"What did you discuss in 'ze boat? If I may ask," Monsieur Roget inquired.

"Things," said James evasively.

"And…?" Kiljoy popped up, poised to hear a good sad story.

"I have to think."

His mind churned through all that he'd heard. It was the way Norman had spoken, with such openness and honesty. True, Norman's anger was scary, but not enough to drive him away. Somehow he understood.

James had never known his own father. He'd never even seen a photograph. Not one. His mother had gotten rid of them long ago. *What if my father was a man like Norman?*

"Well, my demi-king! Now you 'ave achieved what 'ze judges required and will return, triumphant! You will be 'ze new King of Average! 'Ze end of a great adventure, *non?*"

"Hmph!" said Kiljoy grudgingly. "How could I be *wrong?*" He ducked back into Roget's pocket to brood.

"Ba-a-aa-nished!" bleated the scapegoat. *"He* took the blame! *He's* responsible?! That was *my* job! My duty! Baa-aa-aa!"

James stroked Culpa's head and put a comforting arm around him. "It's all right, don't worry. You have me."

"Tha-aa-t's a consolation, at least. I will serve you well, to my last breath, James! *Sniff!*" Culpa bowed on his front knees before him.

"Let's stop all this hogwash and get on with it," said Kiljoy. "The sooner we get this over with, the better."

"You're right," James teased, "...for once. Let's get going."

They found the middle-of-the-road and headed back to Average.

"When you are king, perhaps you could pardon 'ze old king? 'E was a good man, I think. A little scary, but nice. Ah! I cannot wait to see you crowned King of Average, my demi-king. I salute you!" said Roget. "I am so very proud for you. We all are!"

James should have been satisfied. He had accomplished his task with relative ease, but something still bothered him. Soon he would be King of Average. King James the—the what? King James the Not-So- Terrible? Somehow it was a letdown.

Suddenly it came to him. He stopped in his tracks.

What if I found Norman's son and daughter and brought them back together again? A family once more!

CHAPTER 18

A Change of Plans

"WE'RE NOT GOING back to Average!" he announced.

Kiljoy was out of the pocket like a shot, incredulous. "What are you saying? You practically have the crown of Average on your head! What now? Afraid?! Of course, I should have known."

James related his encounter with King Norman, recalling everything they had discussed. It was one thing to lose a kingdom, but it must be unbearable to lose the love of your children. (With the possible exception of his own mother, who probably wouldn't notice one way or the other if James stopped loving her; for anyone else it would be unthinkable.)

Ever since James could remember, he had longed to have a normal family: a father and mother, a brother and sister. Alas, his mother was all the family he'd ever known.

But here was King Norman. A good man, a failed king, and a failed father separated from his children. Children he loved. If he reunited them, James would finally have found a way to make *someone* happy. He cherished the thought.

"King Norman has children. We are going to find them and get them back together as a family," James declared.

Kiljoy was hysterical. "Why on earth would you do that? It's crazy! It's preposterous! That's not part of the deal!"

"Well, I'm going to try anyway."

Kiljoy jabbed his finger at James. "You are stalling! You know you'll make a terrible king and you'll be a miserable failure like Norman. Oh, no!" Kiljoy suddenly moaned. "That means we'll all be banished! What have I gotten myself into?"

"Don't worry, I'm going back, but this comes first."

"More adventure! *Merveilleux!*" cheered the optimist.

"Haven't we had enough excitement for a lifetime?" argued Kiljoy.

"Now you listen, you little beetle. If Demi-King James wants to do something nice for someone else 'zen 'zat is what we will do!" Roget turned to James, beaming. "A most excellent idea!"

Kiljoy threw up his hands in defeat. "And just how are you going accomplish this... this *folly*? It's pure FOLLY!"

"I haven't thought it all out, but—"

"Oh, ho!" proclaimed Kiljoy, strutting around. "A half-baked plan by a half-baked king! Just great!"

"Be quiet," snapped Roget. "James is right! It will be thrilling! Daring and *heroique!*"

"Then it's agreed," James said. "We'll take the extra time before going back to Average." He raised his arm in a rally. "For Norman!" James shouted.

"*Pour* Norman!" Roget chimed in.

"Poor US!" said Kiljoy, climbing back into Roget's pocket.

Culpa asked, "James, you *are* still going to be king, aren't you? Average ne-ee-ds you!"

"Yes, yes. I know! I know!" James insisted. "But first, this."

James pulled out the scraps of paper he'd found in Norman's tent and read them. "The first thing Norman's son would do is look for his twin sister."

"How do you know that?" asked Kiljoy. "A little bird told you, I suppose."

"Wraawk!" A loud screech sounded from above and they all looked up. High in the sky, a black speck descended rapidly. As it got closer, James could see it was the little blackbird with the orange-tipped wings. It landed deftly on James's shoulder and bobbed up and down. "Not me. Wrawk!"

"You keep following me," said James. "You helped me escape the Shadow."

"I do what I can, and go where I'm needed," the bird said, flapping its wings and fluffing its neck feathers.

"'Ow fortunate you were flying by," Roget remarked. "Just like 'zat. Out of 'ze blue!"

"It's not so much luck," cawed the little bird. "It's my nature, you might say. I'm sure you've heard of me."

"No," James confessed.

"You mean you've never heard of the 'little bird'?" It fluttered its wings again and stuck its shiny black beak in James's ear. "I'm the one worth listening to."

"Oh!" James brightened. "*You're* who they mean when they say 'a little bird told me'!"

"Precisely!"

"Are you 'ze same birdie they say to watch when taking a photograph? 'Watch 'ze birdie'?" Roget asked.

"That's my brother. And despite what you've heard, we do *not* flock together."

"Can you tell us where we can find Norman's children?" asked James.

The little bird shook its head. "I know a little about a lot, but I don't know everything."

"King Norman's son wrote that he was going to get as far away from Average as he could. Any idea where that might be?"

"The Unattainable Mountains are the farthest thing from Average," said the bird.

"Then that's where we'll go," said James.

Kiljoy swooned and hit the ground with a small thud while a grim look came over Roget's face.

"'Ze Unattainable Mountains. 'Zey are very, very far," warned Roget.

"Too far!" added Kiljoy, coming to. "Impossible!"

"Nothing is impossible!" Roget contradicted.

"You've got to be kidding me." Kiljoy glowered at his partner.

"Well, maybe not impossible," Roget maintained. "But definitely improbable!"

Culpa spoke up. "They are the most dangerous mountains in the world, James. Practically no one's been near them! It's too-oo-o much for an average person."

"Maybe Norman's children didn't get that far, then, either," suggested James. "I say we head toward the mountains and see if we can't find them and bring them back to Norman."

Roget took off his bowler hat, grabbed James by the shoulders, and planted a quick kiss on each cheek. "*Un beau geste!* A beautiful gesture. You are wonderful, my demi-king!"

"Bite your tongue!" Kiljoy yelled. "He's not supposed to be wonderful, just average, remember?"

James thought aloud. "There has to be someone somewhere who's seen them and knows where they've gone.

We've been down the middle-of-the-road, but that will never get us above Average. Where do we start?"

"So that's it?" cried Kiljoy in one last attempt. "That's your plan? Go somewhere you've never been, find someone you've never met, and get them to do what they obviously don't want? What kind of a plan is that?!"

"Now, now *mon ami* Kiljoy! It is an adventure! *Viva les possibilities!*" Roget cajoled.

"You'll regret it," Kiljoy moaned in a squeaky voice. "It'll never work and I can't wait to say I told you so!"

"Oh, yeah?" James challenged. "What do you say, little bird? Will it work?"

"Wwrawwk! How should I know? I'm no fortune- teller!" said the bird. "I'm instinctual."

"You can say that again!" said Kiljoy, pinching his nose. "Phewww-wee!"

"There's not much to go on," James admitted. "Wait a minute! I remember King Norman told me he sent his daughter to a school near Superior."

"There's Lake Superior," said the little bird, still perched on James's shoulder. "But Superians don't talk to strangers. It's beneath them."

"That's no help." James turned to the little bird. "Can you tell us anything?"

"Try the Flatterlands," it chirped. "But be careful. Don't believe everything you hear."

"If that's the case," said James, "why bother?"

"Rumors abound there. Look for a gossip," said the bird.

"Gossip. Got it," nodded James.

The little bird hopped down and scratched in the dirt with its beak to peck out a trail leading from where they were to the Flatterlands and on to Lake Superior.

The bird pecked at a mark on the outline of the lake.

"Serenity Spa; it's a good place to go if you get discouraged."

James thanked the little bird. It launched into the air and streaked away, its squawk echoing in the distance as it vanished into the hazy blue.

James mused aloud, "He shows up out of nowhere just when you need him."

"A-aand then he's gone again in a flash!" added Culpa.

Kiljoy popped from Roget's pocket and shook his fist at the sky. "Show-off!"

CHAPTER 19

The Flatterlands

THEY MADE IT to the River Maunder by nightfall and managed to get across by appearing to dawdle through the night. They took naps in shifts; James and Roget twiddled their thumbs while the others slept. Kiljoy stayed perfectly still and silent, expecting the river to engulf them at any moment. By midmorning, they had put a good distance between themselves and Average. Culpa pestered everyone to save their strength and insisted they all ride him.

"If it is all 'ze same, *mon chevre*, I prefer to walk," replied Roget in his most charming voice. "I need 'ze exercise. And no offense, but you are not 'ze most comfortable of beasts to ride."

James silently agreed.

The little goat dug his hoof into the dirt in protest, but grudgingly conceded.

"'Ow very understanding of you, *mon chevre*. You are very patient with us," said Roget.

"And how very sincere you are, sir," said a deep, silky voice directly behind him. "My, my, chivalry and civility becomes you."

Spinning around, Roget saw a man exactly his height, wearing a similar waistcoat, cravat, vest, and derby. James and Culpa jumped in surprise—the man had appeared out of nowhere. Roget and the man regarded one another.

The man bowed low and flashed a winning smile.

"You startled me," said Roget. "I did not see you come up."

"That is perfectly all right," replied the man, smiling so broadly his eyes crinkled into a squint. "A man such as yourself must have much on his mind. I'd venture to say you have a great many better things to do than notice a brazen admirer like myself, who dares come so close to get a better look at his hero."

He bowed graciously and doffed his hat. Roget returned the bow, doffing his hat too, saying, "Of course not, but 'ow nice of you to say so."

"Oh, get off it!" snapped Kiljoy, popping out of Roget's vest pocket. "He's after something!"

A little man popped up out of the vest pocket of the other man. He was pocket-sized, just like Kiljoy. "That's the spirit! No beating around the bush! Blunt! To the point! Decisive!" he said, extending his hand. The Kiljoy- like clone had a sniveling smile, a large pointed nose, and a little bald spot on the top of his head surrounded by wisps of hair.

Kiljoy regarded his counterpart with suspicion. "Who are you?"

"I'm just like you. A concerned friend who tries his best to keep his comrades out of trouble. The name is Gilroy. And this," he indicated his larger alter ego, "is Thaddius W. Gladhand."

"My card," said Gladhand, proffering his card, exchanging it for one of Roget's.

The card read "Thaddius W. Gladhand, Sycophant. Purveyor of Plaudits, Palaver, Puffery and Public Relations."

"You two could be brothers!" James remarked, comparing the two standing side by side.

"So could Kiljoy and Gilroy," observed the goat.

"We try," confessed Gladhand. "We enjoy emulating those we admire."

"It's the sincerest form of flattery," said Gilroy from Gladhand's vest pocket.

"So, we're in the Flatterlands?" ventured James.

"Perceptive! Exactly," exclaimed Gladhand. "I must say, I admire your powers of observation. They are indeed keen. You are quite the sharp and canny young man. And your companion! Oh, my! Never have I seen such a fine specimen. Capricorn: agile and surefooted," he gushed in the most sincere tones.

"I'm a scapegoat!" protested Culpa.

"And a terribly good one!" said Gilroy. "I've heard of you. You're a royal dupe! And I mean that in the best sense of the word."

Culpa nodded graciously. "Thank you."

James explained, "We're on a quest. But what I'd like to—"

"A quest! How noble! How exciting!" exclaimed Gladhand.

Culpa added, "It's a quest for James to become King of Average."

Gladhand gasped. "King of *all* of Average? Amazing!"

"I wonder if—" James tried again.

"An odyssey! It's positively mythic!" Gladhand continued effusively. "Imagine, the next King of Average in our very midst!"

"If I could only—" James attempted once again.

"Please! Say no more! You must let us receive you in a more appropriate manner! Our small way of expressing our appreciation. It's my job as the official welcoming committee. Follow me to our humble little hamlet. This way, if you please."

Before anyone could utter another word, Gladhand was off. Roget and Kiljoy, Culpa, and James were swept along behind.

They rounded a bend and came into the village. A sign on the main street read "Welcome to Nobbling. You deserve nothing but the best!"

Out of nowhere a huge marching band greeted them, beating their drums. People crowded the street. Banners proclaimed "Long live the next King of Average!" and "We Love You!" and "You are the Greatest!"

Throngs of people threw confetti, cheering for the newcomers, "Hooray! Thank you for coming!" and "Oh, and how good looking!" "What a nice boy!" "What a handsome, well-dressed man!" and "That's *some* goat!"

James and his little band were overwhelmed. They walked down the street, waving and smiling at their adoring fans. Children ran up to them begging for autographs. They scribbled their names on scraps of paper and patted the happy children on their heads, sending them on their way, surprised and pleased at how little it took to give them so much pleasure.

"Ahh! 'Ow wonderful to be so appreciated. This is *fantastique!*" yelled Roget over the cheers.

"Finally, some long-overdue notice for all my hard work and suffering!" declared Kiljoy.

"I don't deserve this, rea-allly!" bleated the goat halfheartedly, smiling and nodding his head in recognition.

The marching band blared as the raucous procession made its way down the street.

James looked this way and that, trying to take it all in. He smiled so hard his cheeks hurt. He couldn't help it! His smile kept growing and growing while his head swam with the compliments heaped upon him.

Then the crowd rushed forward and hoisted the four travelers onto their shoulders. They carried them to the town hall, an official-looking brick building with two white columns framing highly polished, tall, dark double doors. Wide stone stairs lead to the entrance. Ascending halfway, they turned and waited while everyone cheered some more. "Speech! Speech!" cried the crowd.

"My friends! My dear, dear friends," began Roget. "It is with extreme pleasure I come to the Flatterlands with my brave companions in search of—"

"Bravo!" the crowd yelled back. The applause was deafening. Roget held up his hands to quiet them, but the cheering just got louder.

"'Zis is a bit much!" whispered Roget to James.

"I agree," said James.

"Oh, stop it you two!" Kiljoy objected. "You just don't know how to take a compliment. Look! They *love* me!"

Thaddius W. Gladhand stepped up on the porch and quieted the crowd.

"I would like to express our heartfelt appreciation for your visit," he said to James and his companions.

"I have here a declaration," he said, taking a scroll from a collection of them on a tray, "that certifies that *you* are the bravest, most intrepid person we've ever encountered,"—he handed the beribboned parchment roll to James—"and *you* are the person with the sunniest disposition we've ever met,"—he handed a scroll to Roget—"and *you* are the most long-suffering and patient, underappreciated being in the entire world," he said, as he handed Gilroy a small scroll to give to Kiljoy.

"And last, but certainly not least, the most gifted scapegoat! Stubborn, steadfast, loyal, and valiant." He handed the last scroll to Culpa, who nibbled and pulled at the ribbons, gingerly unrolling the proclamation.

"May I say something?" James persisted.

"Not now, dear boy," Gladhand said, looking at his watch. "You must be tired from your long journey. We can talk in the morning. I'd like to offer you a free night's rest in our five-star hotel, the Indolent Arms. Walk with me."

He led them down the street to a large two-story yellow clapboard building with a wide porch along the front. Several nicely dressed men and women sat on the porch in rocking chairs. They wore flimsy tissue paper crowns. The strange thing was, they had their backs to James and his companions, but their heads were completely turned around, facing James, Roget, and Culpa. They smiled serenely and waved polite hellos over their shoulders.

Several small, round-shouldered, pointy-nosed attendants in white coats ushered James and Roget and Culpa into chairs and gently but forcibly sat them down, putting blankets on their laps, asking "Are you comfortable?" The attendants stood behind their chairs plumping soft pillows and urging James and Roget to lean back and rest. James thanked them over his shoulder.

Several more punctilious porters arrived to stand behind them, covering their shoulders with soft shawls and placing paper party crowns on their heads. James was handed a lemonade and a copy of the local newspaper, *The Nobbling News*.

"Thank you," said James, still craning his now-stiff neck over his shoulder, overwhelmed with all the attention.

"Did you hear that? He thanked *us*! Incredible!" Gladhand announced to the crowd. A cheer rose from the crowd and then, all at once, they dispersed.

James, Roget, Culpa, and Kiljoy remained on the porch with the backward-headed guests. James didn't want to call attention to the fact their heads were on backward, but he couldn't help but stare. The guests occasionally nodded a polite hello whenever one of them caught James gawking.

Soon Gladhand returned. After a quick hello he said, "Thank you for a wonderful afternoon. I'm sure we'll talk again—soon!" Gladhand bowed and took his leave.

James was left with several unanswered questions on the tip of his tongue.

Other than having their heads on backward, the guests seemed very content. James and Roget sipped their lemonade and relaxed in the comfortable chairs.

Kiljoy hung his skinny legs over the hem of Roget's pocket and luxuriated in a soft square of blanket a waiter had given him. Culpa stood on his chair contentedly munching his party hat, the newspaper, and the stuffing from the cushion. "Delicious!" he declared.

James didn't know what to think. The parade was fun. The lemonade tasted good. He opened The Nobbling News, but the headline read, "No News Is Good News," and, in fact, most of the pages were blank. James searched for any news whatsoever, when an ad caught his eye: "Grapevine Detective Agency: Muckraking, Eavesdropping, and Investigation. We make your business our business. Martin A. Blatherskite, proprietor."

"Here's an ad for a detective agency," said James. "Let's see if this Mr. Blatherskite can help us. I don't think Mr. Gladhand is really interested in anything other than making us feel welcome."

"And what's wrong with that?!" barked Kiljoy. "I find Gladhand and his friend utterly charming."

"I don't think he's going to help us," said James.

"I agree," mumbled Culpa with a mouthful of stuffing.

"Let us retire to our rooms to freshen up before we set out, shall we?" Roget suggested.

"Good idea," agreed James, balling up his paper crown and heading for the entrance. The others followed.

They went through the front door, but to their surprise, they found themselves outside again. There was actually no "inside" to the hotel. The building wasn't a building at all, just a façade propped up with long braces. James and his companions looked back through the entrance to the front porch where the other guests still rocked contentedly, smiling and waving.

"Not very accommodating, are they?" James mused.

"On 'ze surface, yes. But that is 'ze problem."

"I should have realized it was a sham when we got here," groused Kiljoy.

"*Oui*. 'Zey turned our 'eads just like 'zey 'ave done to these poor people," said Roget, referring to the backward-headed guests of the Indolent Arms Hotel. "Too much flattery makes you see only what you want to see, and not what is, *n'est-ce pas?*" a newly enlightened Roget remarked.

James, Roget, and Culpa left the shawls, finished their lemonade, and waved good-bye to the poor souls who seemed content to sit in their rocking chairs like zombies, aimlessly waiting for more attention.

CHAPTER 20

Martin A. Blatherskite, Private Eye

MARTIN BLATHERSKITE sat in his shabby office, a lone brick building on the outskirts of Nobbling. The brown wood desk had seen better days. The bottom drawer appeared to be stuck and the desktop was strewn with back issues of *The Nobbling News*. Its crossword puzzles were half- done and the mostly blank pages had hundreds of doodles scribbled on them.

"Norman the Unexceptional had kids, eh?" said the detective, looking up from his desk at James, Roget, Kiljoy, and Culpa. "N the U. Not a bad King of Average from what I heard. Did nothing very interesting to speak of... until now. Disappearing without a word—now *that's* interesting. I'm surprised nobody's gossiping about it. If they were, I'd have heard about it."

Blatherskite's forehead furrowed. He had a long, pointy nose, a weak chin, and his bald pate gleamed with sweat as he sipped noxious liquid from a chipped coffee mug. He smelled like three-week-old gym socks.

"You're not a Flatterlander, are you? Because we need facts, not flattery," James said warily.

"I'm not a Flatterlander. Nope, I'm a Stinker."

"I'll say!" said Kiljoy, turning his face downwind.

"From the Neitherlands, originally. Things were rotten there, so I moved here to set up shop." He laced his fingers behind his sweaty head and leaned back. "Find Norman's kids, huh? Big job, I don't mind tellin' ya." He put his feet, which had a strong cheesy smell, up on the desk.

"Can you help us?" asked James.

"Depends," said the detective.

"On *what*?" demanded Kiljoy.

"Can you afford to find out?" Blatherskite leaned forward, all business. "My kind of work requires certain expenses."

"'Ow much do you need?" Roget offered.

"'Ow, much... I mean, *how* much do you have?" Blatherskite leaned further forward, eagerly licking his lips.

"Eighty-two dollars and seventeen cents in cash, and—"

"That'll just about cover it," said Blatherskite, snatching the money from Roget and stuffing it in into his pocket.

"Great!" said James. "When can we expect to hear some news?"

"Tut-tut! Patience," Blatherskite replied. "Don't you know that patience is a virtue?" He smiled and winked reassuringly at James, taking a loud slurp from his putrid cup.

James was having none of it. He crossed his arms and waited for an answer.

"Soon," said the detective. "First thing I gotta do is investigate places around Superior. I've got a friend who's a guard in Uppity. They're a very exclusive high-class bunch. They love a good skeleton in the closet. If there's any dirt on this Unexceptional kid, they'd know about it. Folks'll talk more freely when they know there's a scandal brewing. Could be the talk of the town! It'll spread like wildfire."

Blatherskite, pleased with the opportunity to spread a good tittle-tattle, rubbed his hands together in anticipation. "I know a great rumor when I hear one! Meanwhile, you have the easy job."

"What's that?" asked James.

"Get an audience with King Onus. See what he knows."

"In Acc-u-u-si-a-aa-aaah?!" Culpa exclaimed.

"Exactly!" Blatherskite stuffed Roget's money in his pocket, led them all to the door, and began pushing them out of his office.

"How will we contact you?" James asked. "...and vice versa? The little bird?"

"I never use him," said Blatherskite. "The grapevine! That's how to get ahold of me. Start a rumor—anything you like—and I'll hear about it. That's how I communicate with all my clients, strictly by rumor. Well, I got what I need. Thanks. Good-bye." Blatherskite gave one more gentle shove and slammed the door in their faces.

"That's a fine how-do-you-do," groused Kiljoy.

"I think it is not such a fine 'ow-do-you-do," a very annoyed Roget objected.

"I was being... Oh, forget it!" Kiljoy threw up his hands.

"I think we've been cheated," said James. "I'm going back."

He opened Blatherskite's office door, ready to demand clarification, but the detective was gone.

The backdoor was wide open. On the desk was a note that read "~~On vacation~~ OUT ON BUSINESS."

CHAPTER 21

Hearsay

ONLY ONE ROAD led away from Blatherskite's office. It split into two roads at a stand of trees, one heading west and the other heading north.

James had no idea which one to pick and the little birdie was nowhere in sight.

With butterflies churning in his stomach, James acted as if he knew what he was doing, hoping to keep everyone's spirits up. "Well, as someone once said, 'Go west, young man.' So let's go west."

Soon they came to a cluster of wooden buildings reminiscent of a bare-bones town in Old West America: a barn, two or three storefronts, and a dusty main street. A wood sign read, "Welcome to Hearsay—Population: None of your business!" It was eerily quiet. There was no one in sight.

As they came closer to the storefronts, the travelers heard the happy sound of voices coming from a building at the far end of the street. Drawing nearer, they distinctly heard laughter, the clink of glasses, and the strains of a honky-tonk piano. The sign above the door said, "The Fault Line Saloon and Emporium."

James peered through the window. He saw a large woman in a fancy dress smiling as she delivered a tray of delicious-looking fountain drinks to a group of gruff and filthy men. They wore moth-eaten hats and bandanas.

"What do you see?" asked Roget.

"Looks like some prospectors having drinks."

"They're dirt miners," said Culpa.

"Dirt miners?" asked James.

"They dig up dirt on people," Culpa said, "and sell it to gossipmongers."

"Maybe they'll have some dirt for us," James mused. "Let's go in."

Before Kiljoy could utter a word of protest, Roget and Culpa followed James inside.

The group of miners stopped mid-laugh and eyed the newcomers warily. The waitress went over to the player piano and threw a lever. The music halted.

James found a seat at an empty table and Roget sat down next to him, politely tipping his derby to the lady. Culpa trotted over to a potted plant and tentatively nibbled at it, unnoticed.

The woman cast an eye in their direction and sauntered over to the table, her petticoats rustling under her full red skirt. James continued to stare at the dirt miners, who stared right back.

"What'll it be?" she asked.

"Root beer?" James asked.

"Nothing for me," smiled Roget.

The woman retreated behind the bar and drew a frosty mug of root beer from a tap.

James nodded a greeting to the men at the next table. The dirt miners raised their eyebrows and exchanged curious looks. They nodded back.

The woman returned to the table with the frothy mug. "Here you are, dear. That'll be fifty dollars."

"Fifty dollars!" shouted James and Kiljoy in one voice.

"In gold, if you have it," she said.

"If you do not mind, Monsieur James, on *moi*! I will gladly buy you 'zis little refreshment," said Roget. He'd given all his cash to Blatherskite, so Roget reached into his breast pocket for his checkbook and, with a flourish, started to write out a check. "To whom do I make 'zis payable?"

"Cash only," snarled the woman.

"But, but we do not 'ave such a sum...."

"That ain't *my* fault! Boys! We got us a situation!" she said.

In a rush the miners pounced on James and Roget and hustled them onto the street.

Culpa looked up from the half-eaten potted plant.

"Baaa-aaa-aaa-hhhh." He ran after them, calling out to the dirt miners, "Whatever it is! Pleee-aaa-se! It's my fault! Let them go!"

The dirt miners froze dead in their tracks, staring in disbelief at Culpa, head down and ready to charge.

"A scapegoat!" the first miner uttered, in awe.

"An honest-to-gosh scapegoat!" said the second. "I thought they were extinct."

"We're rich, boys!" hollered the third.

They leapt at the little goat, grabbed him by the horns, wrestled him down on the ground, and swiftly got a rope around his neck. They marched down the street with Culpa in tow.

James and Roget ran after the kidnappers. "Let him go!"

The three miners ignored him. It was no use trying to rescue Culpa by force. The miners were big and mean.

"Where are you taking him?" asked James.

"Accusia. We're gonna sell us a genuine scapegoat to King Onus."

"He's *my* goat," said James.

"Finders, keepers," said one of the dirt miners while the others sniggered.

"This is terrible!" cried James.

"*Non!* It is a good thing! Don't you see? We will follow 'zem to 'ze king!"

Not far outside of Hearsay, they came to a sign with a large finger pointing out directly into their faces. It read simply, *Accusia*.

They followed the dirt miners into the courtyard of a sprawling fortress. The walls were built with rough-hewn logs sharpened at the ends. The logs were dry, cracked, and weather-beaten. The gardens had all gone to seed and the patchy lawn was overgrown and choked with weeds.

James and Roget saw one of the miners enter a large door in the main house at the center of the compound. He returned smiling with a sack of money. He motioned for his two companions to bring the goat. James and Roget walked right in after them.

CHAPTER 22

Accusia

THE GREAT HALL was gloomy, dark, and smelled of moldy chocolate, sweet and musty. Piles of candy wrappers and Popsicle sticks lay strewn on the tattered royal purple carpet. Shards of smashed plastic toys that had been swept under the rug crunched under their feet. At the end of the carpet sat an ornately carved wooden throne. Behind it hung a green-and-black tapestry emblazoned with the same large imposing pointing finger.

King Onus of Accusia sat on the throne with his arms folded.

James was surprised and heartened to see that he and the king were about the same age.

An oversized crown perched crookedly on Onus's head, being stopped only by his ears from ending up around his neck. He wore a striped green-and-black polo shirt with a white collar, black jeans, and black high-top sneakers. He was very round and squat, and his narrow little eyes were fastened on James.

He pointed a finger and the three dirt miners snapped to attention.

"Bring them over here 'tho I can get a better look!" the king said with a very slight lisp.

"You're just a kid, like me," said James, smiling.

"No! *You're* just a kid! I'm a king!"

"If I may say," began Roget, "'e *will* be a king—"

"You be quiet! I'm not talking to you!" screamed Onus.

"—very soon," Roget trailed off weakly.

Onus turned his attention back to James.

"What are you doing here? I only wanted the goat. Don't tell me. He's your scapegoat and you want him back. Ha! Not a chance."

"Just our luck, the King of Accusia is a loud-mouthed brat," Kiljoy muttered to himself from Roget's pocket.

"What was *that*?" Onus whirled back to Roget.

Kiljoy ducked out of sight.

"Nothing! Nothing, Your Highness. Nothing at all," Roget stammered.

"Are you calling me names?" he asked threateningly.

"I said it," Culpa lied.

"It just slipped oo-ou-out." King Onus turned his attention to Culpa, standing behind James and Roget. He slipped off the throne, hiked his pants up to his large midsection, and waddled down from the platform.

"'Tho it was you, huh?" Onus shoved past James and Roget to appraise Culpa. "Kinda puny, aren't you? My last scapegoat was twice your size. You think you're worth what I paid?" Onus flashed a wicked smile. "Let's see how you take the blame for your friend calling me a brat. How's this?"

He kicked Mayor Culpa hard, on his rear end, jolting the little goat.

"Stop it!" James shouted. "He didn't do anything to you!"

"He's a scapegoat, stupid!" said Onus. He kicked the goat again. Culpa bore it well and bleated piteously enough to satisfy the king.

"Cut it out," James warned.

"Or what?" challenged Onus. He puffed out his chest and bumped James with his belly, taunting him.

"Bully!" James seethed through gritted teeth.

Onus came nose to nose with James.

"Shut up, you! I'm the *king*!"

With a malicious sneer, he shoved James so hard he fell back over Culpa onto the floor. Onus let out a cackle and a snort. The dirt miners nodded and laughed too, encouraging the royal brat.

"'Zat was not very nice," said Roget, helping James to his feet.

Fearing that catastrophe was imminent, Kiljoy jumped from the vest pocket and made a run for it.

"Oh, no ya don't!" one of the miners said, grabbing Kiljoy and presenting the squirming pessimist to the king. Panic made Kiljoy swell up like a small blowfish. The miner held him by his skinny arms, his legs swinging, kicking in the air.

"Calm down, calm down," Onus said quietly. "I'm not gonna hurt you! I'm not gonna hurt anybody."

A relieved Kiljoy immediately deflated and allowed himself to be set down on the armrest of the throne.

Delighted, King Onus grabbed an empty jelly jar from the debris piled next to his throne and scooped Kiljoy into it, clapping on the lid, trapping him like an insect. He picked up a small screwdriver and violently brought the point down on the lid. Kiljoy dodged the dangerous stabs as Onus punched several holes in it and set the jar on the arm of his throne.

"Hey look, everybody! I have a new pet!"

The three grizzled miners smiled and nodded their approval while edging closer to the door with their loot, ready to bolt.

"Take the goat to my room and tie him to my whipping post!" The three miners bowed, grabbing the bleating scapegoat, and made a rush for the door.

"Not you, Toothless!" Onus called to the last miner.

Toothless stopped at the door, his shoulders sagging. The grizzled old miner plastered an ingratiating smile on his face and slowly turned around. "Yes, your high and mightiness?"

Onus crooked a pudgy finger, summoning him forward and commanding him to stand guard over his new treasure. Then he turned his attention back to the others.

"Why *did* you come here?" he asked. "Never mind. I don't have anyone to play with at the moment so you'll stay and keep me company."

"We can't stay," said James.

"I'm not asking. I'm tellin'!" the king hollered.

James spoke slowly in measured tones, holding his temper. "That's not why we're here."

"Oh? Then why *did* you come?"

Though still fuming, James decided to give diplomacy one last chance. James continued to speak as politely as he could. "You see," he said, "I had this idea to be the most average kid in the world and the Council of Judges in Average—"

"You think *you're* going to take the place of Norman the Unexceptional? *You?* Don't make me laugh."

"Well, I'm going to try," said James, reaching his boiling point. "But before I do that, I'm going to find King Norman's children."

The chubby king's expression changed. "Those traitors!" His chin quivered and he seethed, practically snorting through his nose. "Get them out of here! Throw them in the dungeon!"

James expected several more guards to appear, but there was only the lone prospector, Toothless.

"Beg pardon," Toothless ventured, "it's crammed as it is—"

Onus turned purple with rage. *"SHUT UP AND DO IT!!"*

Toothless shook his head and obeyed. "Come with me." He took James and Roget by their shirt collars and dragged them to the door.

"Kiljoy! My compatriot! What about my friend?" Roget asked.

"He's mine now," said Onus.

They looked back at Kiljoy, standing in the jar by the throne, banging away, his tragic cries muffled by the glass.

CHAPTER 23

The Dungeon

THE DOOR SLAMMED SHUT with a thunderous thud. It was pitch black. As James grew accustomed to the dark, he saw they were in a dank cellar. Hallways branched off in various directions. There were at least fifty people huddled by the hard-packed earthen walls. Some were silent and brooding. Others argued, and still others protested, declaring their innocence.

They bickered constantly and whispered, "Shh! Not so loud!"

"Someone'll hear you then you'll get it." It sounded like a disgruntled, argumentative hum.

"It's not my fault, it's yours!"

"No, it's not! Don't blame me for your mistakes!"

"I didn't do anything!"

Some crouched, sleeping with their heads cradled in folded arms. Others slumped as if they'd been waiting for years. Some sat hugging their knees.

James and Roget made their way through the crowd to a slightly less populated alcove.

A shadowy figure moved toward them—a dirt miner. He wore the same dusty hat and bandana worn by their captors. "You must be the strangers who brought Onus the new scapegoat. So, he got tired of you already?" he drawled. "It doesn't take long these days."

"Who're you? How do you know about us?" asked James.

"I get wind of things, even down here. Can't tell you how. Professional secret. Zeke's the name. Used to be a dirt miner. I'm also a bona fide gossip."

"Are those stooges that King Onus bosses around your friends?" asked James.

"Used to be," Zeke said ruefully. "When all the juicy gossip dried up, they started running out of people to tattle on to Onus. They got hold of my stash of dirt 'fer themselves and ended up telling tales 'bout me just so they could stay on Onus's good side, if he ever had one."

Roget spoke. "'Zat is disgusting, to betray your friends."

"It was bound to happen, there just wasn't enough dirt to go 'round," said Zeke. "Onus accused and jailed just about everyone who hasn't fled. Most of what's left of Accusia is in here now. Soon he'll have no one to blame. What did he accuse you of?"

"I don't know."

"Doesn't matter," said Zeke. "We get blamed for everything ever since he lost his last scapegoat."

"Well, he 'as got 'imself a new scapegoat now!" Roget slapped his hands to his side indignantly. "And someone he can complain to who complains almost as much!" The optimist's eyes watered. He removed his monocle and dabbed it gingerly with his handkerchief. "Poor Kiljoy."

The crowd began murmuring. "He's got a scapegoat, you say?"

"Is it true?"

"His name is Mayor Culpa," James explained. "He was sent to find a new King of Average and found me."

An excited buzz shot through the crowd. The Accusian prisoners gathered around James and Roget, peppering them with questions. A young girl made her way through the anxious throng. She wore a tattered blue tunic over a soiled white dress. Her lank blonde hair hung to her shoulders and her long bangs came down to just above her pale gray eyes. James was struck by her loveliness; it was the first time any girl had ever struck him as pretty.

"Mayor Culpa found you?" she said. "I raised him from a kid."

James stared at her in disbelief. "Y-you're King Norman's daughter?"

She nodded. "I'm Marie the Extra-Ordinary."

"*Mon Dieu!* 'Ze Princess of Average!" Roget's monocle popped off his face.

"Your father told me—" James started.

Zeke cut in, "Let's find somewhere more private to talk. This is valuable information. No sense givin' it away for free." He guided James, Roget, and the girl down a narrow corridor and through the honeycomb of the dungeon.

"My brother's here, too," Marie said.

"This is great!" said James. "It didn't take us long to find them after all, did it Roget?"

"Hmm? *Oui,* 'ow very lucky for us," he said halfheartedly.

James noticed how lost Roget looked without Kiljoy in his pocket.

Marie led James, Roget, and Zeke to a dark corner of the dungeon where a boy sat glaring at the wall. He was all arms and legs, lanky and rail thin. He also wore a tattered tunic in the shade of blue that James realized was the official color of Average, tied at the waist with a rope. He had long, straw-colored hair that hung down over his eyes as he bowed his head.

"This is my brother," the girl said. "Jerome the Ordinary."

"Hello," said James.

The boy didn't move. His jaw was set, lips pressed together in a grim frown. His arms were folded and he glared at the wall.

Zeke took James aside. "He's a sulker. Some of 'em down here get like that. He pouts all day long."

Jerome remained stonily silent, arms tightly folded, his expression unchanged. Marie shrugged.

"Do not despair, *mon ami,*" said Roget, patting his shoulder. "We 'ave come to help."

Jerome angrily tore his shoulder away and Roget backed off. "*Pardonnez-moi.*"

James understood. He, too, used to sulk. Sulking was a quiet way of being angry. You gave the silent treatment in order to punish your persecutor, expecting them to be concerned and if they were, you did what Jerome just did: repel any attempt at consolation to hurt them more. James had used it on his mother but it never worked. He would storm into his room when she screamed at him and slam the door to get her attention. Then he'd sulk for hours waiting for her to come and apologize. She never did. Eventually, James realized it was pointless.

"I met your father," James said.

"I don't have a father," Jerome hissed fiercely.

Undeterred, James pressed on. "He's so sorry you ran away."

"Yeah, right,"

"No, really. He's in exile. All alone by Lake Inferior."

"That's the first good news I've heard since I got here," Jerome said, keeping his eyes glued to the wall.

At least he's talking, James thought. He tried putting a solicitous hand on Jerome's shoulder, but Jerome jerked it away, got up, and pushed past James with a shove.

"What's your problem?" growled James, his own anger flaring, and shoved back.

Jerome swung at James and both boys fell to fighting. They wrestled each other to the floor, flopping around, getting in ineffective, poorly aimed punches, each struggling to get the upper hand without success.

Marie and Roget ran in to break it up, but Zeke held up a hand.

"Let 'em have at it."

"But 'zey will kill each other!" Roget protested.

"I won't let it get that far," said Zeke. "They're just blowin' off steam is all."

"I am not so sure," said Roget, holding a worried hand to his mouth.

Zeke edged closer to the squirming boys and stood ready to break it up if it got nasty. It did not. Both boys fell back exhausted, Jerome glaring at James and James glaring back.

"What do you want?" said Jerome, breathing hard.

"To help!" said James, his chest heaving, gulping for air.

"Why?"

"Because," said James, pausing to catch his breath, "your father needs you."

Jerome stared hard at him, giving nothing away.

"He's sorry for how he acted. He told me."

Jerome just glared.

James rubbed a hand down his face, frustrated. How could he get through to this stubborn boy that his father was truly suffering?

"*Excusez-moi*," said Roget, interrupting. "I think maybe King Onus 'as called for us."

He nodded his head that they should look behind them.

Toothless stood at the end of the hall pointing a nasty-looking shotgun at them.

CHAPTER 24

Kiljoy's Revenge

"**ONUS WANTS** to see you," Toothless said. "Let's go."

"Howdy, Toothless. That toy shotgun ain't real, you know," Zeke pointed out as the prospector approached.

"I know that. But they didn't," Toothless sighed. "You just couldn't resist another tattle, could you, Zeke?"

"What about you, Toothless? It was your tattling that got me here, remember?"

"You're right, and I'm sorry 'fer it, Zeke, but that was business, and business is bad. You know how it is," Toothless apologized with a shrug.

"Havin' a good time up there with the king 'n all the money?" asked Zeke bitterly.

"No," admitted Toothless. "It's terrible. I don't hardly get a chance to relax or nothin' 'cause of that big fat pain-in-the-butt!"

"So! I'm a pain-in-the-butt, am I?" shouted Onus.

Everyone froze. King Onus stood at the end of the hall, hands on his hips. Behind him loomed an enormous Kiljoy; he was so big he had to crouch to avoid hitting his head on the ceiling. The once-pocket-sized Kiljoy glowered at everyone.

"Kiljoy!" exclaimed Roget. "You are all out of proportion! What is 'ze matter, *mon ami*?"

"Don't talk to me, you loudmouth!" roared Kiljoy. "We're through!"

Roget gasped. He looked as if he'd been struck in the chest.

Onus leveled his gaze at Toothless and advanced on him. "Well, now, my good old faithful Toothless, you and your tattletale friend can just stay down here together and tattle on each other to your heart's content! You're fired!"

Toothless, finally having had it up to his eyeballs with Onus, moved threateningly toward the chubby boy-king, wanting to wring his neck. But the hulking pessimist moved to protect Onus and grabbed Toothless by the shirt.

"Lock him in there with the other one!" Onus pointed to a nearby cell. Kiljoy grabbed both men and shoved them inside, locking the thick wood door. The dirt miners banged angrily on the door, calling the king every foul name they could think of.

Onus crossed his arms and smirked. "There! That'll show 'em!"

James edged forward. "Kiljoy, what's gotten into you?"

"The truth!" he boomed. "Nobody appreciates what I do, do they? Well, now somebody does and I've seen the light! I've got a much better job than traveling around with you and that deluded optimist. I'm now Prime Minister of Accusia."

"But… but… *mon ami*, we are a team! Partners! Non?"

"No more pocket preaching for me!" Kiljoy exclaimed, jabbing a thumb at himself. "Find yourself another pessimist!"

Roget was speechless.

James seethed. His eyes shot daggers at Onus as he growled through clenched teeth, "What did you do to him?"

Onus gloated. "I inflated his ego." A smile spread across his face so wide, his eyes looked like slits set into his chubby cheeks. "He's my new best friend."

Just as quickly, the king's face went from gloat to glower. He stuck his face in Jerome's and said in a nasally sarcastic tone, "Jerome here will tell you *he's* your best friend. He'll suck up to you like some Flatterlander, but he's a dirty, rotten liar!"

"You threw my sister in jail! You expect me to hang out with you like nothing happened? You order me to play games and what? Keep letting you cheat because you can't stand losing?" shouted Jerome. "*You're* the liar. You killed your scapegoat and you blamed it on everyone else!"

Several nearby Accusian prisoners gasped and a murmur snaked through the crowded dungeon.

Onus was enraged. He vibrated so intensely, his cheeks shook. "Nobody talks to me that way!" he erupted.

"We do! You spoiled brat!" declared James defiantly.

He stepped up alongside Jerome. They advanced on the child overlord of Accusia, fulminating with righteous fury. King Onus quailed and backed away. Kiljoy stepped in front to shield his new friend and blocked their way.

"You won't get away with it forever!" said Jerome.

"We'll find a way out of this stupid dungeon and when we do, you'll get what you deserve!"

Onus countered, "Oh, no, you won't!" He clutched Kiljoy's large bony leg. "Throw them out! All three of them!" he commanded. "Throw them out for good! Make sure they never come back! I never want to see their stupid faces again! EVER!"

Amid all the shouts and accusations, James spotted Marie edging her way down the corridor to the dungeon's entrance. He caught her eye and smiled, motioning for her to go. She returned the smile and disappeared up the steps and into the palace.

The giant Kiljoy dragged James, Jerome, and Roget out of the dungeon and straight to the door of the fortress, shoving them into the pouring rain. He slammed the door in their faces.

Jerome pounded violently on the door. "Send out my sister!"

"And Mayor Culpa!" James shouted, also pounding.

Nobody answered.

Roget was a broken man: his shoulders slumped, his head hung to his chest, and his monocle dangled from his lapel. His once-sharp, pointed moustache unwound and drooped. He began to shrink and his once-tight- fitting vest and jacket now hung loosely on his sodden shoulders.

"I'm not leaving without Marie!" Jerome pounded again.

"We can't stay here, it's pouring," said James. "We'll have to come back for them."

Roget continued to shrink as if the rain was melting him. The optimist stuck his thumb in his empty pocket and shrank even further.

"Don't worry, Monsieur Roget," said James. "We'll think of something."

Roget took comfort from James's attempt to buoy his spirits and stopped shrinking. He looked up at James and said without conviction, "What? Me worry? Never!"

CHAPTER 25

Jerome

JAMES, JEROME, AND ROGET ran toward a stand of trees and brambles in the middle of a meadow. They spied a dense thicket and crawled through the bushes where they found a small open space in the center. Thankfully, the leaves overhead acted like a leaky roof, softening the downpour. Soon, fading daylight sifted through the leaves as the rain slowed. The air smelled of damp earth. The trio huddled together.

"Maybe we'll think of something by morning," James offered.

Roget was silent. James put his arm around the sullen optimist and said, "Tomorrow's a new day, right, Roget?"

"Hmmm? *Oui*, another day."

They sat quietly for a while. Finally, James asked Jerome how he ended up in the dungeon.

"That's a long story," said Jerome.

"I'd like to hear it," James said, hoping it might spark an idea. Plus, he secretly wanted to know more about the Prince of Average and his sister.

"*Moi aussi*. Me too," Roget added, attempting to buck up. "Tell us of your adventures."

James was glad to see Roget's mood improving.

"So, what happened was, I ran away," Jerome began.

"I know," James said. "Your father told me. I also found parts of the note you left. He tore it up right in front of me."

Jerome gave him a surprised look. "Tore it up?"

"He got angry when I asked about you and tore it up and stomped off," James replied.

Jerome snorted derisively. "See? There you have it!"

"Have what? Can't you—"

"Do you want to hear my story or not?!" snapped Jerome. "Because I'm ready to go back there now and get my—"

"No!"

He's just like his father, thought James. What a temper.

"Sorry. I…" James waited for an outburst from Culpa for blurting an apology then remembered his friend was still in Accusia with Jerome's sister. "Go on. Tell us."

Jerome glared at James before he continued. "Okay, so I headed north to find my sister until I got sidetracked in Nobbling."

"Ah, *oui*. We 'ave been there." Roget nodded.

Jerome let himself chuckle at the thought. "When they heard I was Jerome the Ordinary, Prince of Average, they really went crazy. Parades, celebrations… they were even talking of erecting a statue of me!"

James and Roget exchanged knowing looks.

"They convinced me I could do anything. I didn't know what I wanted to do, exactly. All I knew was that it needed to be something amazing so nobody would call me Jerome the Ordinary ever again."

"What did you do?" James asked.

"I came up with the idea to climb Mount Impossible." Jerome laughed at the absurdity of it.

"*Mon Dieu!*" cried Roget.

"Yeah, I know," said Jerome. "Then I found my sister and told her, and of course she was all for it."

James smiled at the thought of Marie and settled in to listen.

"We headed north toward the Unattainable Mountains and stopped at Uppity. Uppity's quite well- to-do, you know," said Jerome, sticking his nose in the air snootily. "They have a gate to keep out the riffraff. There were big houses in neat rows lining the street. We walked up to the gate and told the guard we needed a place to stay. 'No outsiders allowed unless you're especially interesting,' he said.

"I told him we were far from Average and were on our way to climb Mount Impossible. He said we didn't look like adventurers, and Marie just smiled and said, 'Looks can be deceiving.' Then the guard disappeared down the road and came back with an Uppity family. They were all smiles and fussed and fawned over us then asked us to dinner."

A large drop of water fell from the leaves of the bush overhead and plopped onto the brim of Roget's derby. It had stopped raining. Clouds parted like a curtain revealing the moon, full and shining a beam brightly through the canopy of leaves, illuminating Jerome's face in a pale spotlight.

"They asked you to dinner... Then what?" James prompted.

"They walked us down the street," Jerome resumed. "'The name's Evans. Clement Evans, the Third,' the man said, 'and this is my wife, Marjorie, my boy, Clem the Fourth, and little Clementine.'"

"*Oui?* Go on," Roget said, fascinated. As he leaned in, water spilled from the brim of his bowler hat onto the damp ground. He held out his hand, thinking the rain had started up again.

"'Mount Impossible, eh?' the father said. 'You're quite the heroes then, aren't you?' His wife said 'You must tell us all about it!'"

James's soggy pants bunched at the knees. His leg had fallen asleep and he had to shift to unfold it, massaging it to get the circulation going. "Go on," he said. "I'm listening."

"'After dinner, you simply *must* stay here! We *love* entertaining heroes!' The lady was practically shouting."

At the mention of dinner, James's stomach growled. They hadn't eaten in some time, and he was ravenously hungry. Ignoring his hunger pangs and his wet pants and his numb leg, James put his full attention on Jerome.

"We followed them down the street. The houses were really impressive! They had brass nameplates on the doors. Every other one said 'The Joneses.' There certainly are a lot of Joneses in your town, I said. 'Gotta keep up with them,' Mr. Evans said. 'That's the rule if you live here.' Dinner was delicious. A perfectly cooked roast."

James's mouth watered.

"It was kind of awkward, though. Nobody said anything. They just stared at us, smiling. Finally, Mrs. Evans broke the ice and asked us to tell them about our expedition. I told her we were Jerome the Ordinary and Marie the Extra-Ordinary.

"She looked disappointed. 'Norman the Unexceptional's children? You're *average* then?' she said with a frown. And then she brightened. 'At least we can say that you're a prince and princess. We don't have to say where from. Oh, my friends will eat this up!'"

James rolled his eyes. *Such snobs,* he thought to himself.

"Little Clem the Fourth told us he got all A's on his report card, and his sister Clementine pointed to a picture on the wall; it was a drawing of three tulips and a tree in a real fancy frame. She said everyone tells her that she's artistic. I told her it was nice. Marie and I could hardly keep from laughing."

"Ah! Children! So amusing, *non?*" Roget concurred.

Even though it had stopped raining, they were drenched and chilled. They scooted closer to each other for warmth.

Jerome continued, "Then the little girl shouted, 'We're Uppies!' Her father told her it's not polite to say 'Uppy.' That's what other people called them—the envious ones. Clementine giggled and Mrs. Evans pointed out that Envia was the next town over. 'Our stepsister city,' she called it."

James stifled a yawn. Jerome stopped.

"See what I mean?" he said glumly. "A long story."

"No, no. Keep going," said James. His numb leg was finally waking up, with a serious case of pins and needles tingling as feeling returned.

Jerome leaned forward and spoke with more energy, trying to make his story more dramatic.

"Okay, so, now there we were." He paused for effect. "Mr. Evans said he was very impressed at our being the first Average people to ever attempt Mount Impossible. Then he started bragging about himself. Said he did some climbing in the Unattainables. He told us once he and some friends made it all the way to Mount Irony and showed us a rock on the mantle. 'Ironic ore,' he said. It looked just like a regular rock, the kind you'd see in Average, and I said so.

"'That's the irony,' Mr. Evans said, punching me hard in the arm. 'Pretty good, huh?' Then he asked what our plans were after making it to the top."

"What do you mean?" asked James.

"He meant, what was the reason for the climb? Fame, or fortune… you know? Well, I did have a reason but it sounded stupid; I didn't want to be called Jerome the *Ordinary* anymore. I was embarrassed, so I didn't say anything."

"What's wrong with being ordinary?" James interrupted.

"What?" Jerome looked up.

"I said, what's wrong with being ordinary?" James repeated, somewhat affronted.

"You mean be just like my father?" scorned Jerome. "Not me."

James let out an exasperated groan. "Why can't you understand…? Your father is—"

"Stop talking about my father!" Jerome snapped. James shook his head wearily. "If you could only see—"

"Do you want me to go on or not?!" Jerome challenged. "'Cause I can stop right now…"

"Sorry." Once again, James looked for the absent Culpa, who'd have been upset to hear him apologize.

Again, his heart sank at his friend's absence.

An uneasy moment passed before Jerome settled back down.

"Um, where was I? Oh, yeah. I said, 'I really didn't know why exactly.' That's when he got upset and started lecturing me about ambition. 'You are going to do the most impossible thing in the entire world and you have no idea why or to what end you'd exploit it?! Leverage it! Impress them and you'll have 'em eating out of your hand!'

"Then Mrs. Evans scooped up the plates and sent the kids to bed. She walked Marie and me to the door saying dessert didn't turn out well and she was sorry and all. She said she had forgotten that their guest room was full of camping gear and the maid hadn't been there. I asked if we could stay on the couch, and she wouldn't hear of it. 'Try next door,' she said. She pushed us out the door and slammed it shut and turned off the porch light."

"Outrageous! 'Ow rude!" Roget exclaimed.

"Yeah," agreed Jerome. "Marie and I headed toward a little park at the end of the street, but the guard came by and said Uppity ordinance something-or-other forbade vagrancy. He showed us out and locked the gate behind us. So there we were, back where we started."

"And then what 'appened?" asked Roget, breathlessly.

"Lucky for us, Marie and I had bedrolls and some warm clothes. We walked for about an hour and came across this run-down fortress. This chubby kid was playing all by himself in front."

"Onus," Roget scoffed.

"Right. We told him what happened in Uppity, and he laughed and said they were a bunch of losers. I said 'Rich losers,' and he said, 'So what? I'm rich. I'm the king.'

"Marie said that she thought Onus the Terrible ruled Accusia. The kid said that Onus the Terrible was his father, and had recently passed away. He wasn't very broken up about it. 'I used to be Onus junior but now *I'm* the king,' he said. 'So I'm Onus the Great, okay? Onus the Great.'

"He said we could stay with him and took us around and then he showed us his room. He had a whipping post with a really big scapegoat he called Old Faulty tied to it. The poor goat was in really bad shape, beaten to within an inch of his life."

James and Roget gasped.

"Yeah," Jerome agreed. "Marie told him that she had a pet goat once and she'd try to help him. But it was too late. Old Faulty didn't make it."

"*Horrible!*" cried Roget.

James pictured Culpa tied to that whipping post and the beatings he would take. "We've got to get Mayor Culpa out of there!"

"And what about Kiljoy?" Roget stood up. "Prime minister to 'zat brat! 'Ow could he do such a thing?! His 'new best friend'… Outrageous!"

"Not for long," Jerome predicted. "Cross Onus once and that's it, you're his enemy. He's gotten rid of practically everyone in Accusia. There's no one left to blame."

"Except for Mayor Culpa!" cried James.

Jerome slammed his fist into his palm. "What're we going to do?!"

"*Oui*, what?" Roget asked.

"I don't know," said James, defeated.

"Me neither," said Jerome, totally frustrated. "It's hopeless."

"Do not say that, *mon ami*," begged Roget.

The only good thing in all of this, James thought, was seeing the twinkle rekindle in Roget's eyes. "It will all work out for 'ze best. We shall think of something! There is always a way."

They wracked their brains for a plan, fruitlessly, late into the night until sleep overtook them.

CHAPTER 26

Kiljoy's Adventure in Accusia

THE CHILL EARLY LIGHT of morning woke them. They got up slowly, damp with dew, discouraged that they were no closer to having a plan for rescuing Culpa and Marie.

"*Zut alors!* I must 'ave slept sitting up. I am so stiff!" Roget laboriously raised himself up by his cane, stretching from side to side, front to back, and left to right.

"Jaa-aa-aa-mmes!" sounded a familiar bleat. "Where are you?"

James let out cry of happiness and shot from the bushes. Culpa came galloping toward them across the field, followed by Marie.

Jerome ran to meet his sister and they embraced, laughing and crying with joy.

Roget cheered, "'Ooray!"

James hugged the little scapegoat mightily. Monsieur Roget smiled and clapped for them while scanning the meadow for any sign of Kiljoy, but his old partner was nowhere in sight. Roget sighed while his hand unconsciously once again searched the vacant pocket Kiljoy once called home. He gasped, jerking his hand out, surprised—no, overjoyed!—to see a tiny Kiljoy clinging to his gloved thumb with a grin so big it looked like a banana under that silly bulb of a nose. He tossed Kiljoy in the air triumphantly.

"Aaaaaggggghhh!" Kiljoy landed with an "oof," ordering him loudly to never do that again as he jumped into the safety of his pocket. He grabbed the edge and poked his head out, letting his nose drop in front, fully reinstated to his former size and temperament.

Roget grabbed Culpa by the horns and planted a big kiss on each shaggy cheek, in the French custom, and gave the same to Marie. James wanted to greet her likewise, but held his hand out instead. Marie threw her arms around his neck and hugged him tightly with a glorious laugh that made James's heart pound.

The happy laughter and greetings went on until they were spent. For a long time, no one spoke. No words were needed. They basked in each other's presence and beheld each other in contented silence. All but Kiljoy, who couldn't let such a nice moment pass without making a sour remark.

Then, as if on cue, they all spoke in a rush: "What happened?!"

"How did you escape? Tell us!"

"*Oui!* What 'appened?!"

And so on.

"Kiljoy, why don't *you* tell them?" Marie prompted, poking at Roget's waist.

The pessimist peeked over the rim of the pocket, his eyes shifting left to right and right to left. Guilt was written all over what could be seen of his face. Culpa trotted up to Roget and stood practically eye level with the tiny pessimist and nudged his drooping nose with his own.

"Yes, Kiljoy, tell u-uu-s?"

All eyes went to the former Prime Minister of Accusia.

"It's not important. We have better things to do," Kiljoy deflected, searching their faces for a reprieve.

No one budged.

"Oh, all right!" he relented. "I saw you leave and I was trapped in that jar! What a catastrophe! I was ready to explode, but I couldn't. The jar was so tight. I watched Onus throw a huge temper tantrum. He knocked over chairs and threw his shoes and broke anything he could get his hands on. He was out of control!"

Kiljoy paused and glared at them. "None of that mess back there was any of my doing, you know!" he said. "I warned everyone, didn't I?"

"Go-o-o on!" Culpa urged. Kiljoy squirmed. He was not letting Kiljoy off the hook just yet. "What happened next?"

"Well, he cried and cried and cried. Then he kicked the throne, stubbing his toe. He hollered and hopped about on one foot. 'Serves him right,' I thought. I couldn't help but laugh. Pretty funny, right?" Kiljoy waited for a commiserative chuckle from his audience. Silence.

"Well I thought so, anyway. But my laughing made him mad. 'What's so funny?' he asked. I know a catastrophe when I see one and I started to expand, but the jar wouldn't break. Every part of me was pressed up against the glass. I was squished tight. I looked like some kind of science experiment. Then Onus forced a laugh. 'HA-HA! Now that's funny!' As I squirmed, he unscrewed the lid and pulled me out of the jar like a rabbit from a hat. Then he held me up to his face. 'You think it's funny when somebody gets hurt?!'"

"Oh-oh," said Roget.

"Now you were in for it!"

Kiljoy held up a hand and looked crossly at his friend. "Not at all. May I continue?"

Roget beamed and nodded, "But of course! By all means!"

"I apologized, '*No*, it's not funny. I'm very, very sorry, your highness.'" Kiljoy looked at their skeptical faces and implored, "What was I going to say? 'Sure! Real funny?' He'd've killed me!

"He put me down on the arm of his throne and started massaging his toe. I tried flattery like old Gilroy would've. 'It's maddening when people don't understand,' I said. 'I know what it's like. How hard it is. Believe me.'

"Onus climbed up on his throne and started talking nonstop. He told me how everybody had it in for him and how mad it made him. Then he asked me what I was doing with a bunch of losers. *HIS* words!" Kiljoy said defensively.

"I said something like, 'Nobody understands, do they?'"

James rolled his eyes, as did Jerome, Marie, and Roget.

"And that's about it. I guess the old saying 'misery loves company' is true. We talked and complained about everything. It felt good! None of you take me seriously. He took me into a room with a strange contraption and handed me a hose connected to it and told me to put it in my mouth."

"*Sacre bleu!*" Roget's hands flew to his face in horror.

"Don't be ridiculous," said Kiljoy. "I'm here and I'm alive, aren't I?"

"Of course you are, *mon ami*! Forgive me. I am spellbound! You tell a good tale."

The compliment was not lost on Kiljoy, who preened before regaining his cantankerous composure.

"Now, for the last time, may I go on with my story?" he asked tetchily.

"Onus told me this would make me feel even better than I already did. He attached a funnel to this contraption and as he pumped, he spoke into it. He said how loyal and strong I was and what a natural-born leader I was. And he said *terrible* things about all of you." Guilt spread across Kiljoy's face. "He kept funneling me with all this malarkey and I started to believe it. Then I began to grow—but not catastrophically! Confidently. I grew so full of myself it felt... it felt good! There, I said it. He made me feel important. Not only did I get bigger, I got stronger with every word he fed me. He told me that he was my only friend and I, his." Kiljoy saw Roget was obviously hurt, and he quickly looked away.

"But 'ow could you believe that nonsense?!" Roget said. "'Ave not we always been honest with each other? Are we not best friends? Why, *mon ami*? Why?"

Kiljoy couldn't face his friend. He bowed his head and mumbled some excuse about being a victim of an inflated ego.

James, Jerome, Marie, and Culpa clucked their tongues and shook their heads.

"Well, you know the rest. He appointed me Prime Minister and made me his new bodyguard." Culpa snorted disdainfully.

"So you're going to make it all MY fault now?" Kiljoy accused Culpa. "You always give James a break, but you won't give me one?" The little scapegoat grudgingly gave Kiljoy's nose a nuzzle.

"Look what 'appens when you don't 'ave me around," Roget admonished.

Kiljoy was sufficiently contrite.

"But we still don't know how you all got out!" Jerome said.

"Yes!" James asked. "I'm dying to know."

Marie said, "I can tell you that."

CHAPTER 27

Marie and the Goat

"**I SAW ALL OF YOU** dealing with Onus and Kiljoy," Marie explained, "and I took a chance to slip out and rescue Mayor Culpa."

Culpa chimed in, "When she came in I said, 'Mari- ee-eee-e-e! What are—'"

"Shh! Let Marie tell it," said James.

"So-orry," Culpa said. "My fault for butting in." The scapegoat sat on his haunches and looked contentedly chastened.

James smiled and patted him on the head. "Go on, Marie."

"I told him that my brother and this boy were holding off Onus and a big ogre they called Kiljoy."

Mayor Culpa burst out, "'Prince Jeroo-oo-ome? Kiljoy?' I te-e-ell you, I was incredulou-us!"

Everyone shushed the butt-inski scapegoat. "So-o-rry. Couldn't help myself," the goat said sheepishly. "Go on, Marie. It won't happen agai-ain."

Marie lovingly stroked his neck. "Then we heard King Onus and Kiljoy coming down the hall. I had to think fast. 'Lie down,' I said to Culpa. 'Pretend to be very sick! Hurry!'"

What a smart girl, James thought. *Smart and brave.* He beamed with admiration, but she didn't notice as she was well into her story.

"Mayor Culpa fell over and began bleating and moaning, pretending he was in terrible pain. King Onus and Kiljoy came in and Onus shouted at me. 'What are you doing with my scapegoat? How did you get in here?'"

"I told him I'd heard in the dungeon that he'd gotten another scapegoat and just had to come see. 'I wasn't able to save Old Faulty, but I might be able to save this one.'"

"Jerome told us about you and Faulty," James said.

"Um-hmm," Marie acknowledged. "I said I felt so guilty about not being able to save Faulty and that's why I escaped—to help him. 'But this scapegoat is sick,' I said. 'Very sick! He's taken on the blame for all of Accusia. And he did it for you so you could release your subjects and have them back to lord over.' And I asked him, 'Isn't that what you really want?'"

"Brilliant!" exclaimed James.

"'Poor little Mayor Culpa has taken on too much too soon,' I said. I told Onus that Mayor Culpa needed to be much bigger and stronger. And that once he was, I would stay and take care of him and Onus would never ever need another scapegoat again."

"Did he think you were telling 'ze truth?" Roget inquired.

"Of course he did!" shouted Kiljoy from Roget's pocket. "You forget I was there, too. The brat bought it hook, line, and sinker! … And so did I," he admitted with some chagrin.

Roget clapped his hands. "*Remarquable!* So clever. *Exceptionnelle!* No wonder you are Marie 'ze Extra-Ordinary! *Très bien!*"

Marie allowed herself a little bow before continuing her story.

"Then Onus turned to Kiljoy and told him he'd have to stand in for Mayor Culpa. Everything would be his fault until he had a proper scapegoat."

Kiljoy popped up and interjected, "I was shocked! SHOCKED! *I knew it!* I said to myself. I should have known it was too good to be true… *Mmmnnfff!*"

Roget pressed a gloved finger over Kiljoy's mouth. "Ignore 'im. Please continue, Marie."

"Onus ordered Kiljoy to show us out to the meadow," Marie said.

Kiljoy managed to get out from under Roget's thumb. He popped back up and shouted triumphantly, "I showed them the way out, all right! I opened the door and we *ALL* ran!"

By now the sun was shining, warming them as they made their way from the bushes into the green meadow dotted with wild clover, dandelions, and yellow and white daisies.

"Bravo, Marie! Bravo! An incredible adventure! I saw 'ze whole thing as if I was there! What marvelous storytellers you all are!" said Roget, smoothing the wrinkles out of his still-damp coat and brushing a few leaves from his shoulder. Jerome, Marie, and Culpa thanked Roget, and even Kiljoy restrained himself from brushing the compliment aside with a nasty remark.

"*Finalement*, we are ready!" said Roget.

"Ready for what?" asked James.

"To return to Average triumphant! You will reunite Jerome and Marie with their father and become 'ze new King of Average!"

Jerome and Marie were both taken aback. "*WHAT?*"

James winced. "Everything happened so quickly, I didn't get a chance to explain. You need to come back with me."

"NO!" they both shouted.

"That is *not* gonna happen!" said Jerome, stomping off.

James called after him, but it was too late. Jerome had stalked away to the edge of the meadow, his back to them, furious.

"He's just like his father," said James.

Marie touched his shoulder. "He's right, James. We can't go back. Not ever," Marie sadly said. "I'm not allowed and Jerome won't do it."

For the first time, James saw pain and sorrow in her eyes. She was hurting badly. Until then he'd only seen her as smart and helpful. And so pretty.

"Thank you again for saving Mayor Culpa. We couldn't have done it without you," said James consolingly.

"It's all right," Marie said, regaining her composure. "I wasn't going to let him suffer in Accusia."

"But your father is suffering, too—terribly. He's out there all alone at Lake Inferior."

Marie scowled, unmoved.

James debated whether to tell her about her father's wanting to drown himself in the Sea of Doubt. "Your father... he only wanted what was best for you."

"He only wanted what was best for himself!" scorned Marie. "He said I was too conceited and too smart for my own good. He never liked me. Everything I did, he either hated or ignored. He never let me go out. I humiliated him. All I ever got was 'Don't show off and don't try so hard; be more like your brother.'" Her chin quivered.

"He was afraid," James explained.

"Afraid of what? Me?" Marie's voice rose. "Ashamed is more like it."

Jerome returned with a solemn expression and grabbed his sister by the hand. "C'mon, Marie. Let's go and let James get back to Average."

"Wait!" James shouted. He grabbed Jerome's sleeve.

"Where will you go? What will you do?"

"None of your business!" said Jerome, yanking himself free.

"You're right. But wait! Please," James begged.

"Don't leave yet. Look, we've all had a narrow escape and a long night. I'm cold and hungry. None of us have had any time to rest or think. Let's find some food and get our bearings. Then you can figure out where you'll go and what you'll do. That makes sense, doesn't it? It wouldn't be good if you up and left now."

"A little rest would do us good!" Roget remarked.

Then he exclaimed "Serenity! 'Ze little bird said something about Serenity Spa! After all 'zis excitement, it would be a good place to go, *non?*"

"That's an idea," James said. "Any objections?"

Jerome and Marie liked the idea and everyone waited to see what sort of snarky remark Kiljoy would make.

"Don't look at me," said the pessimist. "I'm too worn out to think."

CHAPTER 28

Serenity Spa

THEY WALKED NORTHEAST, avoiding the Flatterlands and Uppity, and headed toward Serenity Spa on the west side of Lake Superior.

Roget proudly took the lead, with Kiljoy asking from his pocket, "Are we there yet?" every four or five minutes. James walked up front with Roget, enjoying some pleasant conversation. The optimist pointed out the healthy benefits of a nice walk and how fortunate they were it wasn't raining, and how lucky they were to escape "'zat terrible place."

James couldn't help stealing glances at Marie. She talked easily with Culpa as they walked along. The little scapegoat was almost as devoted to her as she was to him. They reminisced about when they were both kids in Average. The scapegoat looked happier than James had ever seen him.

Jerome slouched along behind them, glumly keeping to himself.

By early evening, they came upon a neatly groomed road leading to a lush, beautiful arbor of blooming vines that spelled "Serenity Spa" in wonderful cursive letters.

The companions passed through the fragrant arbor onto a rolling velvety green lawn that ran to the shorefront of Lake Superior. Here they found a collection of bungalows, each with its own garden of white, pink, blue, and yellow tulips. The windows radiated a golden glow as dusk deepened. The beautiful scene made them all sigh with relief.

 "Hello!" A sprightly man with white hair, wearing a red flannel shirt, yellow suspenders, and blue jeans, emerged from a large cottage by the lakeshore and approached them. His eyes twinkled, and his plump face, rosy cheeks, and snow-white hair made him look like a retired leprechaun.

"Welcome, my dears," he said, "to Serenity Spa. The name's Osgood. My wife, Harriet, is inside making dinner for everyone. You can join us if you like, or eat in your bungalow if you're tired and need time to yourselves. Come! I'll show you to your rooms."

"Wait!" said James. "Were you expecting us?"

"We expect everybody! Now don't worry, we have plenty of room, plenty of room," he assured them. "We're here to take care of all your needs and allow you a fine rest and a pleasant time."

Osgood led them past the cluster of small cottages. "Some nice peace and quiet for some reflection, am I right? That's what we're here for. Take your time and enjoy. When you're refreshed and satisfied we'll discuss the particulars, if it's all right with you."

James was so tired and hungry that everything Osgood said sounded all right with him.

They followed Osgood past the bungalows along a garden path and arrived at a rustic lodge with a sod roof lush with flowers and plants. Osgood motioned for them to come inside and showed them around. There were fruit baskets and flowers in every room. Hot bowls of delicious soup beckoned on their night tables. They ate ravenously. The beds were incredibly soft, and it wasn't long before all the well-fed travelers were fast asleep, blissfully dreaming.

While they slept, the moon rose over Lake Superior and moonbeams spangled the water. Gentle waves lapped the shore all through the night.

The next morning, rested and relaxed, James walked onto the lawn and down to the lake. Marie was already there. They both stood quietly admiring the view.

James tried to work out some way to get Jerome and Marie back with their father, somewhere they could be happy and a family again. He hadn't come up with anything, but hoped Marie might say something to help him figure it out.

"I wish you and Jerome could come back with me to Average. I know you can't. And Jerome? Even if he did want to go back, he won't go without you because you... you're really—" (James wanted to say something especially nice) "—not average, are you? No, of course not. You're Marie the Extra-Ordinary."

"That's what they call me," Marie replied.

"I think you're excellent!" James said in a rush, instantly cringing. He felt a hot blush rise into his face. *Excellent?! What a stupid thing to say!* He held his breath, mortified, waiting for her to burst out laughing. He couldn't look at her and kept facing front toward the lake. The silence grew longer and longer. He imagined she must be biting her lip to keep from laughing. He sprang away toward the shore, praying she wouldn't follow, and hoping and dreading she would. What was the matter with him? What was he thinking?!

Marie watched James sprint away. She started after him but thought better of it and stopped. When James turned back, she waved, and he waved back. James signaled he had to urgently use the restroom. She nodded and headed toward the main lodge.

James sat by himself on a bench near the bathroom, replaying in his head over and over the stupid thing he'd said, thinking now of all the things he should have said instead.

"Ah, *mon ami,*" Roget said, sauntering up to James. "What a glorious day, *non?*"

"It's *too* perfect if you ask me," grumbled Kiljoy, working unsuccessfully to come up with something bad to say about the place.

"It's great," James agreed, glad to take his mind off Marie for the moment.

"My demi-king," Roget said, pointing to Jerome standing by the shore with his hands shoved in his pockets, his shoulders tensed, pacing back and forth. "Monsieur Jerome looks *très désolé*—er, disconsolate. Very sad, *non*?"

James and Roget walked out to Jerome. "What's the matter?"

Jerome threw a rock into the lake, sending ripples across the glassy, calm water.

"Who am I fooling? I can't climb Mount Impossible. I'm no hero." He turned to them.

"Truer words were never spoken!" agreed Kiljoy, relishing Jerome's glum mood.

"What are you saying?" James was surprised.

"I don't know," Jerome admitted. "I don't belong here, above Average."

"Then come back with me," pleaded James.

"No!" said Jerome, emphatically and bitterly. "Never!"

James watched him pull back into his shell like a stubborn turtle, refusing to hear another word on the subject. But James wouldn't let it drop. "You have to believe me. Your father truly—"

Abruptly, Jerome turned and walked away. Roget shook his head. "Tsk, tsk. So stubborn."

"I'm stumped, Monsieur Roget. Should I just leave them and go back to Average by myself and do what I came to do?"

Kiljoy sprang from Roget's pocket and did a little jig on the shore. "Whoopee! Now you're talking! You've come to your senses at last! Finally! Hallelujah!"

James and Roget each watched Kiljoy's celebratory dance and had the same idea. Roget nodded with a wink and slowly moved his cane between Kiljoy's dancing legs and tripped him. He fell spread-eagle into the water. Roget extended his cane and hooked Kiljoy by the neck and pulled him out like a scrawny trout.

"Just look at you! All wet! Come, let us go back and dry you off. You may catch pneumonia, poor fellow."

"*Pneumonia!* Quick! Hurry!" Kiljoy commanded as he dove into the warmth of Roget's pocket. Roget left with a grin, waving toodle-oo to James.

James ran to catch up to the still-brooding Jerome. "You're not sure. That's normal, give yourself some time," James said. "When you decide what you want, things change." *Boy, do things change,* James thought.

Jerome shook his head. "I dunno, I hate being so average. I just want to be really, really good at *something*."

"It's strange," mused James. "All *I* want is to be average, just like you."

"What for? Why be a nothing like me?" Jerome asked.

The "nothing" comment zinged a raw nerve, like a jab to a sore tooth. James bristled. "'Cause," he said tersely.

"Because why?"

"Just because!" said James. "Never mind. Let's drop it."

Now it was Jerome who was surprised. "Okay. Fine."

James quickly changed the subject. "You don't know how lucky you are. What you have."

Jerome looked puzzled. "You have a father—"

Storm clouds gathered in Jerome's eyes and James immediately took another tack.

"I never had a father. It's only me and my mother."

"Same thing," Jerome said.

Not the same, James thought. His mother was nothing like Norman.

"And you have a sister!" James added.

Jerome shrugged. "So?"

"A sister you love, who loves you."

Jerome nodded. "True."

"If *I* had a fantastically beautiful, smart sister like yours…" James bit his tongue. Too late! The heat rose in his cheeks, with the dawning realization that he had a crush on Marie and had just now told her brother—out loud!

Jerome said something but James couldn't hear over the loud roar in his ears from his crimson blush and his pounding heart.

He dashed off as fast as he could toward the bungalow. He was ready to die from embarrassment.

In the distance, Jerome called, "Hey!"

James got to his room, slammed the door, and threw himself on his bed. *What did I just say?!* he asked himself incredulously. He liked Marie, more than a little. His stomach churned. His chest constricted. His brain threatened to implode. Cupid's arrows pierced him like pins in a pincushion.

A soft, cooling breeze blew through an open window and drained the heat from his cheeks. James sat up and stared out the window. Lake Superior was beautiful and soothing. His embarrassment ebbed.

Ding, cling, clang, clong, bong! came the happy sound of the breakfast chimes. "Come and get it!" hollered Osgood.

All the spa guests came out from their cabins and headed to the main lodge. The prospect of food proved the best distraction, and James sprang off the bed, ready to indulge in another scrumptious meal.

Osgood and Harriet had breakfast waiting for everyone. Marie was already sitting with Roget while Kiljoy reached from his pocket to grab a handful of bread. James joined them and Jerome arrived moments later. Culpa remained outside, nibbling on a perfectly baled cube of hay.

They were served a delicious breakfast of eggs, bacon, oatmeal, tomatoes, and rolls. There were juices of every kind on the long table and milk sweeter than anything James had ever tasted.

"Hope you like it, folks!" said Osgood. "Just part of the package here at Serenity Spa."

The dining room filled with a wide variety of guests. Old married couples walked arm in arm. Young newlyweds held hands. A group of ladies from Uppity strolled in, smiling at everyone indiscriminately without once looking down their noses. That was the magic of Serenity. The atmosphere was carefree and relaxed.

James's troubles seemed small and far away. A wonderful breakfast lay in front of him. It was a beautiful day. He had new friends. And there was Marie. That was all right, too, even with the embarrassing turbulence she caused; it was, after all, a nice turbulence. James took a sip of juice and sighed. He just was. And, for the moment, that was enough.

CHAPTER 29

Scent of a Scoundrel

BREAKFAST WAS just about done. Éclairs and fruit plates were set out. Roget cheerfully tried to convince James that every cloud literally had a silver lining.

"That is why raindrops shine," Roget explained.

James could have enlightened the wide-eyed optimist by informing him that clouds were simply water vapor clinging to dust waiting to be drained by changes in the air temperature, but he thought better of it, knowing that bursting Roget's bubble was Kiljoy's only pleasure.

Harriet gathered up the dishes as the conversation continued.

"Am I too late for breakfast?" asked a familiar voice.

"Not at all, Mr. Blatherskite," said Osgood cheerfully, setting a place at the end of the table.

"Blatherskite?" James and Roget said to each other, astounded.

Martin A. Blatherskite came in from his morning swim in the lake, wearing a white terrycloth robe embroidered with the words "Serenity Spa." With the end of the clean towel draped over his shoulders, he blotted the water from his baldpate.

"Good morning! Wonderful day! Water's perfect. I suggest everyone have a swim."

As he strolled by, James pushed back his chair at just the right moment, sending Blatherskite sprawling. James signaled and he and Roget grabbed him, making it appear they were helping him up. As he got a good look at the pair, the detective's jaw dropped and he tried to run. James and Roget held on tightly.

"Found out any juicy bits we could use yet?" asked James pointedly.

"I... er... Oh, don't you worry! I've been hard at work on your case. I... I just needed a little rest, that's all. Yours is a tough case. But, hey! I've got some great information for ya. Good stuff," Blatherskite stammered and blustered, trying to stall while he came up with an explanation. He was caught and he knew it, but his smile was still wide and his eyes were innocent as he tried his best to appear sincere.

"Really? 'Ow wonderful!" Roget winked to James.

Still holding him tightly, James and Roget took Blatherskite outside in an outwardly friendly way so as not to arouse the concern of the guests or the proprietors. Jerome and Marie followed, surprised and curious to see what this was all about.

Once outside, Blatherskite said in a rush, "Now wait a minute, just a minute! What? Did you think I wasn't working for you? Didn't I tell ya I had to interview some folks here? Well, that's what I've been doing."

"What 'ave you found out?" asked Roget.

"Don't listen to him," said Kiljoy. "He's going to swindle you again."

"Me? Never!" protested Blatherskite. "Okay. Here's the news on King Norman's kid." Blatherskite became solemn. "I'm sorry to be the one to tell you. He's dead."

"Dead?" Jerome moved in closer.

"Deceased. Expired. No more. Word is he fell to his death climbing Mount Impossible. Lost in an avalanche, I suppose. No trace of him. Probably never will be," said Blatherskite with sincere finality. "I was just on my way back from Uppity and stopped here at Serenity before I told you, that's all."

"And where did you get this information?" James narrowed his gaze.

"Professional secret, kid," Blatherskite said, smiling. Just then a large white blob of bird dropping landed on Blatherskite's bald head.

There was a cackle and chirp overhead. Everyone looked up to see the familiar blackbird with orange-tipped wings fly by holding something in its talons, laboring mightily to stay aloft. It flew into the leafy canopy of a nearby tree.

Seeing what the bird did to the lying con man started Kiljoy tittering, chuckling, and then laughing. He couldn't help it. His laugh rose to a guffaw and soon he was doubled over in howls. He slapped his hands over his all-too-smiley mouth and dropped into Roget's pocket. He popped back up again with an exasperated look. "This is getting ridiculous! I can't even stay in a bad mood anymore! I need to get outta this place!"

Kiljoy disappeared once more to regroup and sour up.

"Allow me to introduce myself," said Jerome, stepping up to the sneaky snoop from Nobbling. "I'm Jerome the Ordinary, and this is my sister, Marie the Extra-Ordinary. Our father is Norman the Unexceptional, former King of Average, and you, sir, are a liar."

Blatherskite began perspiring profusely. His pungent sweat mixed with the bird's droppings emitted a rank smell.

"Whew! You stink!" Kiljoy said.

Everyone backed away as the odor grew strong enough to wither flowers.

Blatherskite saw his chance. He ran straight for the arbor to make his exit, but as he passed through the trees, the arbor sprang to life. Vines and tendrils reached out and caught him, winding him up in a tangle.

Osgood rushed from the main house and ran up to Blatherskite. "Leaving so soon, Mr. Blatherskite? There's the matter of the bill. Did you forget?"

"No. It's on my bed. All of it. Eighty-two dollars! Keep it. It's all yours!" Blatherskite said, nervously.

"'Zat is my money!" called Roget. "You stole it!"

"I'm sorry, Mr. Blatherskite," said Osgood. "Your bill is five hundred ninety-two dollars and thirty-five cents, plus tax and gratuity, and now, an extra charge for activating my arbor. That comes to seven hundred forty-three dollars even."

"I don't have it," said Blatherskite.

"You don't have it," sighed Osgood. "I'm terribly sorry. We'll have to make other arrangements, then."

"Yes, yes! I'll send it to you." Blatherskite brightened, still suspended horizontally. He craned his neck to come eye to eye with the owner of Serenity Spa.

Osgood shook his head. "I'm sorry, that won't do. You don't have an account with us."

After a moment Osgood inhaled deeply and sighed. He shook his head sadly. "Well, if you don't have it, you don't have it," he said.

"Th-thank you. I'm glad you understand," said Blatherskite, still suspended from the branches.

"We'll just have to take back all your serenity and send you on your way," Osgood said, ushering Roget, James, Jerome, and Marie away from the mysterious plant. As he did, the vines gathered around Blatherskite, holding him in. Tiny tendrils snaked around him, getting into his hair, ears, and nose, even crawling under his fingernails. They suckled at the poor detective. He looked like a caterpillar caught in a strange leafy cocoon.

Blatherskite whimpered. He cried and whined, sobbed, and wept. His eyes darted to and fro, and his shoulders hunched as he shook with fear and despair. Within minutes, he was reduced to a frightened, nervous mass of anxiety. The branches, having consumed his peace of mind, relaxed, and dropped him to the ground.

Blatherskite, looking positively miserable, scrambled to his feet, his eyes full of worry and doubt. He ran toward the hills, moaning. It made everyone who witnessed it uneasy.

Kiljoy climbed out of Roget's pocket and watched with interest as the detective fled the scene.

"He fell to pieces right before our eyes!" Marie said, horrified.

"Not to worry," said Osgood. "Whatever peace of mind he had before he came here will come back to him. We take most of it away to make our point. No freeloaders. Sorry you had to see that. I'm sure you'll need to stay an extra few days to rid yourselves of that unfortunate scene. I feel responsible for disturbing your peace of mind, so I'll discount your stay twenty percent."

"Is there some problem here? It could be my fault! Blame me, blame me!" bleated Culpa as he came up from the lodge, having heard the commotion.

"Wouldn't hear of it, my dear goat," said Osgood.

Kiljoy climbed up to Roget's shoulder and whispered something in his ear.

"Ah, yes. Good point," Roget told Kiljoy. He turned to Osgood. "Excuse me, Monsieur Osgood, but my partner and I are curious. 'Ow much do we owe you for our stay here?"

"So far, for the six of you… hmmm, let me see…" Osgood paused, doing some calculations in his head. "With breakfast, house cleaning, one night's stay times six, minus the discount I extended you… for the six of you it will be three hundred fourteen dollars and ten cents."

Roget gulped. "Would you take a check on good faith? I could pay you in installments…"

Osgood frowned. "I'm sorry, my dears, but that won't do. A check is a promise and they are so easily made and broken these days. Serenity is a rare luxury and quite expensive. I wish there was something I could do."

He snapped his fingers and the vines rustled ominously.

Just then, something glinted in the sun as it fell from the sky, landing a few yards away in the soft lawn. *Thunk!*

The group turned. There, sunk halfway in the grass, was a tarnished jewel-encrusted gold crown. A black, orange-tipped feather fluttered slowly from the sky, coming to rest in the center of the crown.

"Our father's crown!" said Marie. Jerome made no comment.

James bent down to pick it up. A note was spiked through one of the crown's peaks: "*A little bird told me you needed this. I am sorry for everything.*"

James handed the note to Jerome, who read it, crumpled it up, and threw it in the lake.

CHAPTER 30

Serenity Secured

OSGOOD PULLED the jeweler's eyepiece from his eye and held the tarnished crown up to the light. James, Jerome, Marie, Roget, Kiljoy, and Culpa stood across the desk in anxious anticipation.

"These jewels are certainly not the highest quality I've seen. But they're not the worst by any means," Osgood concluded.

"Of course not! They're average! What do you expect?" Kiljoy pounded his fist on the desk.

"The gold is fourteen carat, not twenty-four," Mr. Osgood added, "but I'm happy to say it is more than sufficient."

They were all elated.

"What an extraordinary thing for the former King of Average to do," said Osgood. "You must mean a great deal to him."

James watched Jerome and Marie. They revealed nothing.

"I should tell you that this not only pays for your stay but will allow you many more visits," Osgood added. "If you want to take the crown back, there would still be the matter of the bill."

James shook his head. "Norman meant this for his children. I'm sure I'll get my own."

"Well, then. If you'd like to leave it on account..."

"We may not be able to come back for a while," James said.

"If ever!" Kiljoy emphasized. Serenity was definitely not his cup of tea.

"Ah, yes," said Osgood. "You're off to become the new King of Average. Congratulations, by the way."

"Thank you," James said in a low voice.

"Not very enthusiastic, are we?" Osgood replied.

"This is where we say good-bye," Jerome interrupted. "We've got to get going."

"Oh? Where to, if I may ask?" Osgood inquired.

Jerome paused, exasperated. He slapped his hands against his thighs. "I don't know!"

"Hmmm. Do I detect a little uncertainty?" Osgood diagnosed. "Listen, seeing as your father's crown is on account and your bill is settled, I have something extra for you." He clapped Jerome on his shoulder. "I'd like to give you some presence."

"What kind of presents?" objected Kiljoy with narrowed eyes and a furrowed brow. "What are you trying to pull?"

"No, no, my dear pessimist, you misunderstand." Osgood opened a drawer. "I'm offering Jerome this amulet. It's called a Presence Stone. Presence, not presents."

He held up a translucent stone suspended from a leather lanyard. "It gives the wearer presence of mind. Helps one savor the moment, if you will, and lets you see with detached and clear vision the here and now, unobstructed. It is very rare."

"What good is that?" derided Kiljoy. "It's not the present that's the problem. It's the future, which is bleak and getting bleaker, if you ask me."

"*Non*, my friend. 'Ze future is always bright, full of promise!" Roget contradicted.

"Oh my, you truly are a pair," Osgood chuckled.

Jerome took the amulet. "Thank you." He put the lanyard around his neck, and for a moment, no one could take their eyes off Jerome. He seemed to stand a little taller; he looked relaxed and poised.

"Do you feel all right?" Roget asked, noticing the change.

"I feel fine," Jerome smiled. "Great, in fact. It's just that everything looks a little… different."

"Different how?" asked James.

"Sharp. Fresh, more like. It's like I'm seeing things for the first time. Look at this desk." Jerome bent down to examine the desktop. Everyone leaned in to do the same. The mahogany gleamed in the golden light of the lamp. The detail of its iridescent grain was beautiful.

"It is indeed beautiful. I 'ad not noticed. *Très bien!* Very good!"

"Not interested!" came Kiljoy's reply.

Jerome said, "I'm seeing you all differently, too."

"Different how?" Kiljoy asked suspiciously.

Jerome moved closer to Marie. "I see how much you care about me."

"Of course!" Marie said.

He studied James for a moment, then said, "I see how nice you are, and how generous. You're a good person, James. I'm glad to be your friend."

James smiled appropriately and automatically but the compliment made him uncomfortable. The sinister voice of the Shadow would flatly reject it. "I'm glad to be you friend too," he said sincerely, trying to ignore his discomfort.

Kiljoy popped up and asked, "What about me?"

"I see how constantly worried you are, Kiljoy, and how afraid. And I'm sorry for you."

"Well, don't be!" cried Kiljoy. "All that I'm afraid of is this gushiness getting on my nerves. I'm out of here." He couldn't slip back into Roget's pocket fast enough.

Jerome turned to Osgood. "Thank you, very much. I really appreciate it."

"Not at all, my dear boy. It's the business I'm in." He patted Jerome on the back. "Presence. It's a quality feeling! Serenity's best product. It's always on sale in the Serenity Spa store, but not many notice it." He picked up the crown and deposited it into a large black safe. "Please feel free to stay on as long as you like."

They thanked him and moved outside to discuss their options.

"So, my friend with presence," Roget said to Jerome, "what will you do now? 'Zis very moment?"

"Yes, where to?" James asked eagerly.

"I have no idea!" Jerome said in the next breath but this time with gusto rather than gloom.

"What did I tell you!" exclaimed Kiljoy, jumping from Roget's pocket. The little man strutted around on the lawn, triumphant. "Ha ha! All that foolishness and he still has no idea!"

Osgood spoke up from the doorway. "No idea? Why didn't you say so? I suppose you did before. But now, if you're certain you're uncertain, then what you need is a notion."

"I do?" Jerome said.

"'E does?" Roget's eyebrows widened, letting his monocle dangle.

"Why yes, of course!" Osgood assured them. "Head over to Eureka. It's on the other side of the lake, up in the foothills. Find yourself a nice notion. Eureka's full of them. It may lead you to a good idea and perhaps you'll even find Epiphany."

"Epiphany?" James asked, suddenly very interested.

"A village somewhere high in the Unattainables, or so legend has it," said Osgood. "It's uncharted. People go looking for it and most never find it. Sometimes people stumble upon it accidentally. In Epiphany you'll find insight and transformation. Some say you gain wisdom. You can learn the truth about, well... just about anything. In an instant! It's a special knowledge that comes from who-knows-where or why. Legend has it that the High Epiphanum, a holy man, leads you to it. They say in Epiphany lies your destiny."

"Then let's find Epiphany!" Jerome said emphatically.

"It's no walk in the park, my boy," warned Osgood. "You can look and look your whole life and never come upon it. It finds you, if you're ready for it, and if not, you can easily lose your way. Many seekers have. You might find it easier to start by finding a notion in Eureka. Dig around there for a nice one and see where that leads you."

"All right then," Jerome declared. "I'm off to Eureka to get a notion."

"Me, too!" Marie jumped with joy.

"I'm coming with you!" cried James, without a second thought.

A small howl came from Roget's midsection.

"A new adventure! What could be better? Eh, *mon ami?*" the optimist assured Kiljoy. When there was no answer Roget inspected his pocket. "*Zut alors!* 'E 'as fainted."

"But what about being King of Average?" Jerome reminded James.

"It will have to wait. I'm going with you."

"I'm so glad," said Marie, making James's heart skip a beat.

"Bu-uu-t James. Average needs you! You must come back with me! Baa-aa-aah! I've failed!" the little scapegoat wailed. "I've led you astray! It's all my fau- ult!" He lowered his head and prepared to ram Osgood's desk.

"Not here, my friend." Osgood grabbed the goat by his horn. "Please. Go out and find yourself a nice soft tree or clump of dirt. Can't have you disturbing the guests."

Culpa took off, looking for something he could quietly beat his head against.

"Mayor Culpa is right," said Roget. "You should not risk 'zis. Failure is likely. There is a good chance we will never find Epiphany. Do not ruin your chance to be King of Average, my demi-king!"

James took Roget by the arm and walked him away from the group. He whispered, "Don't you see? Jerome and Marie are so stubborn they have no idea what a good man their father is. It's plain to me, but they don't get it. What if they got the notion I could be right? Maybe I can convince them to come back and rescue Norman from the Sea of Doubt."

"You think?"

"I know!" said James.

"If you say so, *mon ami!*" Roget grabbed James by the shoulders and administered a double kiss on the cheek.

"It's a little weird for me, all this kissing," James said. He tried to remember the last time his mother had kissed him. He sadly realized she never had.

"I do it for 'ze *joie de vivre*! The joy of being alive!" Roget sang out. "I do not know 'ow, *mon ami*, but I am positive everything will work out for 'ze best."

"Hogwash!" hollered Kiljoy, coming out of his swoon.

CHAPTER 31

Eureka

THE NEXT MORNING James and his companions gathered by the arbor. Their genial hosts provisioned them with Serenity Spa souvenir backpacks stuffed with luscious food and other necessities for their journey. As the friends headed north along the shore of Lake Superior, James turned and waved farewell to Osgood and Harriet and the idyllic Serenity Spa.

Jerome and James walked side by side at a steady clip. Roget whistled a tune while Kiljoy moaned and complained about the noise. The louder he groused, the louder Roget whistled.

James grinned from ear to ear. Marie was also smiling. She and James were pleased to see Jerome in such fine spirits. Gone was the formerly sulky, sullen Prince of Average; he'd been replaced by a collected, composed, and relatively cheerful boy eager to find his place in the world. They made good time while Culpa trotted dutifully behind.

By afternoon they were at the top of Lake Superior. The air was brisk, filled with the scent of pine and cedar. The rocky shore was strewn with white boulders flecked with quartz, sparkling pink in the sunlight. Beyond the shore, meadows of tall yellow grass and wildflowers spread over hill and dale beneath a clear, cloudless sky.

A few hours later, the meadows were behind them. The companions climbed up the green foothills toward the stony timberline. The Unattainable Mountains loomed large and craggy, imposing their sawtooth gray silhouette against the deepening blue sky. The highest peaks vanished into misty clouds.

Kiljoy grew more and more distraught, describing in detail every possible horrible outcome of searching for Eureka. "There's a reason they're called the Unattainables, you know!"

Everyone did their best to ignore him.

"No one ever comes back from those mountains! Ever!" Then he added, "You can't get there from here!"

Culpa continued to bring up the rear. The bossy goat had little to say. He trotted along, hoping James would soon make a mistake or a misstep that could be blamed on him, but there was nothing to be blamed for at the moment. He stopped every so often to bang his head on a rock, but butting his head without a good reason wasn't very satisfying.

Roget kept pace with James, and as they hiked, he struck up a conversation.

"Ah, James, You must be so 'appy and excited to 'elp your friends and to accomplish your dream too, eh?"

"I am, Roget!"

"'Ow wonderful it will be to return to Average with such a story to tell! 'Ow you rescued Jerome and 'is sister. 'Ow we stood up to 'zat despicable brat in Accusia and 'ow you 'elped—"

"He hasn't helped do anything but strand us in the mountains, where we'll surely perish from cold and starvation!" Kiljoy grumbled.

"It won't be-ee-e his fault!" Culpa said.

Eureka was farther and higher up than they expected. They found a switchback trail that zig-zagged all the way up, cutting through the pass. When they stopped for a rest, James got a good view of Lake Superior and the land below.

By early evening, they came to a ramshackle collection of rough-hewn lumber cabins. The main cabin had thick plank steps leading to the front door. The sign on the door read "Eureka Mining Co."

James knocked. Roget peered in the window, while Jerome and Marie went to each of the smaller cabins and knocked. There wasn't a soul in sight.

"Everybody satisfied now?" shouted Kiljoy. "You've had your fun. Now let's go back before it's too late!"

James bent down to peer under the porch of the main cabin and dragged out a key he found in the dirt. "Look!"

The key fit into the lock and James slowly pushed the door open. It was dark inside. He cautiously stepped inside; the others followed.

Suddenly the lights burst on so bright, everyone had to squint or cover their eyes.

"SURPRISE! Welcome! Welcome, welcome! You did it! Hooray!" cried several voices.

A jug band struck up a lively rendition of "She'll Be Coming 'Round the Mountain."

James blinked his eyes several times and found himself standing in the middle of a rustic meeting hall. The wood walls gleamed with a fresh coat of pine- scented lacquer, making the dark grain of the blond wood stand out dramatically. The room seemed much larger on the inside than it had appeared from the outside. A balcony with a sturdy railing ran around the room. On it hung a colorful yellow-and-red bunting. The balcony was crowded with people waving, hooting, and whistling. Tables by the wall were piled with loaves of crusty bread, fruits, cookies, and chocolate. Each table held a punchbowl.

Men, women, and sturdy and stout dwarves surrounded James and his friends. Some of the men wore overalls, and some wore brightly colored long underwear. With their beards and grizzled faces, they looked like well-scrubbed dirt miners as seen through a funhouse mirror. Several plump, jolly ladies wore oldfashioned party dresses of satin and velvet, festooned with ribbons and silk flowers, while others wore plain gingham skirts with colorful bibs. In the corner four musicians played a kazoo, harmonica, washbasin drum, and a shovel strung with a few wires. The bassist madly plucked away, keeping time to the music.

James, Jerome, and Marie were taken by the arms and hurled into a square dance. Roget clapped in time while Kiljoy covered his ears. Culpa looked on from the porch, dumbfounded.

The song ended, and they all had to catch their breath. The ladies swarmed Marie and fussed over her, commenting on her plain, dirty tunic and dress, suggesting this or that to "fancy her up."

"...Is this Eureka?" Jerome finally asked.

"That's right! You found it—Eureka!" said a stocky, gray-haired man. His fingers were hooked in the straps of his overalls. He wore a most infectious grin.

"This wasn't at all what I expected," said James.

"Well, what did you expect?"

"I-I don't know," confessed James. "I had no idea what to expect."

"And now you do!" He gave James a slap on the back. "If you ever come back this way, you'll know, won't you? It's always a celebration when someone discovers the key to Eureka!"

A table was set for dinner, and James, Marie, Jerome, and Roget sat down with a few friendly Eurekans. Stew bubbling in a big pot on an old cast-iron wood-burning stove was ladled and served in tin bowls. A basket of rolls went around, and jars of sweetwater were handed out. Everyone could have as much of anything as they liked.

Jerome and James gaped in wonder between courses throughout dinner. Culpa had to be dragged inside. He sat quietly on his haunches and looked around uncomfortably at so many amiable people. He couldn't find a fault among them.

"Who found the key to the door?" asked the gray-haired man.

"I did," said James.

"Well done! Lotsa travelers come by and miss us completely."

"It's wonderful!" Marie exclaimed. "You're all so kind. Such hospitality!"

"Don't mention it," said the man. "The name's Gus. Short for August, which means noble and impressive. And seein' as I'm so short too, just call me Gus. Heh-heh!"

A good-natured chortle went around the room.

Roget spied an attractive woman in a shiny blue dress standing near the stove. She was as round as he was and a bit taller. She had a bewitching smile, beautiful sparkling green eyes, and glowing white hair done up high on top of her head. He strutted up and introduced himself.

"*Bonjour, mademoiselle.* Monsieur Roget at your service." He gave her a gentlemanly bow and handed her his business card.

"How do you do, Monsieur Roget," she said, taking his card. "My name is Hope."

Roget's eyes lit up and he smiled. As a precaution, he quickly buttoned the pocket in which Kiljoy was stewing and buttoned his waistcoat even more firmly around his middle to make an extra layer between Hope and his pessimistic pal. "My favorite name. *Enchanté!*" He took Hope's arm and squired her away to a corner of the room for an intimate chat.

Gus spied the amulet around Jerome's neck. "Nice little gem you got there. Presence, ain't it?"

Jerome nodded.

"We got lotsa that 'round here. I like the way it's set on that leather string," he said. "So what can I do you for? Lookin' to see what sorta notion goes with it or what you can trade it for?"

"Well, not really. I'm looking for something to do," said Jerome.

"To do with what?"

"With me," Jerome answered earnestly. "I'm... that is, since I left home, I don't really know what I should be doing... with my life, I guess. Not a clue! Typical, right?" Jerome offered him a smile.

"Hmmm. Tall order, that one," said Gus seriously. "Normally people have more immediate issues, like solving a formula, a math problem, or a puzzle, or inventing some new thingamabob and such. We supply most people everything from a glimmer of an idea to a notion to a vague idea, and they're happy enough with that and go on their way."

James interrupted, "Can't you give him an idea of exactly what he needs to do?"

"Nope," said Gus. "We just pan the small stuff. It's up to you to find the big ones."

That was disappointing; James had hoped Jerome would realize how much Norman needed him back.

A woman in a lovely yellow dress and red sash entered and approached Marie. "Hello, dear. My name is Faith."

"I'm Marie. How do you do?" Marie replied.

"Very well, dear. Very well. I see your brother is searching for answers. Is there anything we can do for you?"

"I don't think so," Marie said. "We're all here for my brother. He's... well, he's an ordinary boy. You know, average. I think he needs a little reassurance. I'm not as..."

"Uncertain?" offered Faith.

"Yes, that's it," Marie agreed. "I can do a lot of different things. I know I'll find out what I want to do, eventually."

Gus slapped the table. "Well, there you go! That's something we can help *you* with, young lady."

"You can?" Marie asked.

"Really?" added James.

"Ah!" Roget clapped. "Wonderful!"

"You have enough certainty already, young lady. But you could definitely use a notion to point you in a direction. You might find some purpose pebbles lying around," said Gus. "They'll give you an inkling of a career or a calling."

"They're a lovely lavender color," said Faith. "They would go nicely with your complexion." She smiled.

"What about me? What do I need?" asked Jerome.

"You? You need more of an *idea*," said Gus. "Maybe if you go digging in the mine you'll discover one. There are lots of great gems of ideas down there."

"Dig?" Jerome frowned. "Sounds like a lot of work."

"Yep," replied Gus. "You could stay here with us until you strike it. Ya get room and board. We could always use another hand."

"I don't know," Jerome said. "I thought it would be a lot easier than that."

"It can be for some," Gus told him. "For most, it's a lot of sweat and tears. A few come up here and expect to be hit on the head with a bright idea. I'm not sayin' it can't happen, but it's not likely. More often than not, you gotta roll up your sleeves and dig down deep. It's hard work."

James saw Jerome's shoulders slump. He worried Jerome would slip back into sulking and feeling sorry for himself.

"But for a notion or a hunch, just go outside and pick one up. They're everywhere. Just poke around till you find one you like," continued Gus.

James was puzzled. "So you don't sell notions like Serenity Spa sells souvenirs?"

"That's their business, not ours. Nope," said Gus, "around here things are free for the taking."

"How do you know which one to choose?" James asked.

"Oh, you'll know," said Faith with a smile. "One will eventually stand out over the others."

"It's kinda like collecting shells at the seashore. You find lotsa different ones, but there's always one that becomes yer favorite," said a cross-eyed man in a patched orange shirt. Each patch had an unusual design on it. The man's pants were a little too short and held up by one rainbow-colored suspender. The other strap dangled down below his waist. He wore mismatched shoes: one was a heavy leather sandal and the other was a boot with a tall heel, which made him walk unevenly. But through the grizzled stubble on his face, he smiled the same wonderful smile Gus had.

"I had my eye on ya ever since ya got here," he said to James with a rural twang. His eyes were so crossed they converged near the bridge of his broad nose.

James wondered if he could see at all. "Couldn't help but notice you. 'What a strikin' young man,' I told myself the second I laid eyes on ya."

"Me? Striking?" James didn't think he could strike anyone as remarkable.

"Yessir, I can see you have a doozy of an idea! It's written all over you."

"I do? It is?"

"I look for crazy ideas. That's my stock in trade. The name's Slim. Slim Chance," he said, admiring James like a rare specimen.

"I'm James. Pleased to meet you, Slim." James stuck out his hand. "I mean Mr. Chance."

"Slim's fine," he said, vigorously pumping James's hand. "I could take it off yer hands if you've a mind."

"I'm not sure what you mean," James admitted.

"How 'bout a trade? Say for this here." Slim produced a roll of leather. He unfurled a corner of it and James could see it was a map.

"What do you mean? Trade what?" James was curious.

"Your idea. It's a wild idea. I'd like to have it."

"First of all," James said, "what idea are you talking about?"

"So ya want to bargain, do ya? Fine by me," Slim said with a gleeful grin. "Tell ya what. Just give me half your idea, and ya keep the other half. You can still have the map."

"I still have no idea what you're talking about," James insisted.

"Ya have a mind to be the *most* average person in the whole world. I'm right, ain't I?"

"You want *that* idea?"

"I sure do," said Slim. He leaned in conspiratorially. "Where'dya get an idea like that anyway?"

"It just... it came to me out of the blue," James told him.

"Oh, I don't think so, but if ya don't want to tell me, it's none of my business. So what do ya say? A trade for the map?"

"How can you take an idea from somebody?"

"Oh, no! I wouldn't take it," said Slim. "Wouldn't be right." He rubbed his hands together. "I'd love to have it though. It suits me." He gave James a cross-eyed wink. "Don't ya think?"

James was intrigued. "Okay, say I did want to give you my idea. Why is a map such a good deal? What's it worth?"

Slim pulled James close and whispered softly, "It shows the way to Epiphany."

James exclaimed, "Epiph—"

"Shhhhh!" Slim Chance clamped his hand over James's mouth. "Nobody knows I got it."

James remembered what Osgood had said: *"In Epiphany you can get to the truth of things and find your destiny."* What harm would it do to give Slim half his idea in exchange for a map to Epiphany?

"So I can keep half my idea," James said. "And you'll give me the map?"

"Yep," said Slim. "Deal?"

"Deal." They shook hands.

Slim rerolled the leather map, tied it with a piece of string, and handed it to James. "Keep this under yer hat."

"I don't have a hat," said James.

"Well, keep it outta sight. Tell no one." He gave James a slap on the back and strode over to the table to get a slice of cake.

"What about my idea to…?" James started to say.

"To be…" But he had to dredge the thought to the front of his mind. What was his idea again? To be the most average person in the entire world, a feat that would make him King of Average. It struck him as funny. *You can't be the most anything in Average, can you? How would you…?*

James tucked the map into his shirt and mulled over this half-formed idea. It sounded reasonable. Average needed a king and he had been chosen. But he couldn't quite grasp the whole idea anymore. It made his head hurt to think about it.

I'd better not think too hard, he remembered. *Or question everything. Then I wouldn't be average.* He put it out of his mind for the time being. Still, it niggled him to do so.

"James! James! Come quick!" It was Marie calling from outside. James sprinted out the door.

"What is it?" he asked.

"What is what?" Roget and Jerome asked, as they and Culpa came running.

"I have it!" she exclaimed.

"What? What?" they cried.

"A notion! And I think it's a good one," Marie said.

"It's beautiful," said James. "What is it?"

"Forgiveness," Marie replied.

CHAPTER 32

Forgive and Forget

JEROME TOOK THE STONE and inspected it. He gave it a toss to feel its heft.

"Nice, sis," he said, clearly not impressed.

Marie took the stone back and smiled. "I feel so light! I could be a feather in the wind."

James saw how happy she was, and smiled too.

"That is wonderful!" Roget cheered.

"Would you... could you forgive your father, for instance?" James ventured.

Marie nodded.

"Let me see that again," said Jerome. Marie handed the stone back to her brother. "*Hmph*. Doesn't do *anything* for me. Not a thing."

James asked to hold it. It felt smooth and comfortable in his hand, but it didn't inspire him either.

Roget praised it, holding it in his gloved hand as if it were the most precious gem he'd ever seen. "*Magnifique! Breathtaking!*"

"It's just a rock!" grumped Kiljoy.

"Mayor Culpa, you're next. Come have a look at my stone," Marie said. "Mayor Culpa?"

He was gone. Again. James got scared. Last time Culpa disappeared, James had been confronted by the Shadow.

"Mayor Culpa!" James called. "Where are you?" He heard nothing but the wind howling farther up the mountain.

They searched the camp, going through every cabin, even the ones occupied by the other workers. Culpa was nowhere to be found.

James frantically searched the area and discovered an opening in the mountain face. A board nailed across it said "KEEP OUT." James ran to see if his friend was hiding in there.

"Stop!" cried Gus. "Don't take another step!"

James halted. "What's the matter?"

Gus came running up, huffing and puffing. "He didn't go in there, son. Or if he did, it's too late," said Gus. "Look down. But be careful. That's the old mine, and it's a dud. We call it Futility. We stopped diggin' there years ago."

James braced himself by the side timbers at the entrance and stared down into an abyss. The shaft was so deep it was dizzying. It bore down into the earth so far you couldn't see the bottom, only darkness.

"Mayor Culpa!" James called down. "Mayor Culpa!"

"Mayor Culpa! Mayor Culpa, 'yor Culpa, Culpa!" his echo came back.

"Oh, no!" James cried. "Could he have…? Did he fall…? Is he…?!"

"I'm sure he had more sense than to go in there," Gus assured him. For a moment, Gus searched around on the ground. He picked up a helpful thought. "I have it! He's a scapegoat, and goats are sure-footed. He must have gone up the mountain."

"*Oui!*" agreed Roget, coming up from behind. "'E must 'ave gone up there!" Roget pointed to a steep, craggy slope shrouded in mist high above.

"I've got to go get him!" said James, ready to climb despite his fear.

"Hold on!" said Gus. "Those high peaks are treacherous, son. You've made it safely this far, but it's not wise to go any farther."

"But Mayor Culpa," James cried, "I need him!" Jerome and Marie held him back and tried to comfort him. Roget did too. They led him to the porch of the main cabin and sat him down. Several Eurekans crowded near the door seeing James was near panic.

"It will be all right, I am sure," said Roget. "Maybe 'e went down 'ze mountain and not up."

"You don't know that for sure," Kiljoy butted in.

Jerome scanned the area near the shaft and was drawn to an unusually black, shiny rock. The surface glinted in the moonlight. "Look at this." He picked it up and handed it to James. James instantly stopped crying, wiped his eyes and nose on his sleeve, and inspected the rock with interest.

James and Jerome were both totally absorbed with the rock. They finally looked up to see Roget and Marie staring at them.

"Why are you looking at us like that?" asked James.

"Yeah, what's the matter?" added Jerome.

Marie and Roget looked confused. "My demi-king," Roget began, "you 'ave lost your scapegoat and you were so upset!"

"Was I?"

"Upset about what?" Jerome inquired.

Marie stared at them, disbelieving. "Are you two all right?"

"Yes," said James. "Fine," said Jerome.

"They've got hold of a bit of oblitterite," said Gus. "Makes you forget."

"Forget what? Everything?" asked Roget.

"A piece that size, mostly your troubles," Gus replied.

"Get it away from me!" shouted Kiljoy, jumping down and scuttling under the porch like a frightened cat.

"It wears off pretty quick," said Gus. "It's gettin' late. I'll open one of the empty cabins. You can bunk there for the night."

"*Merci beaucoup.* Thank you very much," said the optimist with a tip of his bowler.

Roget coaxed Kiljoy out from under the porch and back into his pocket while they set up the bunks with the blankets Osgood had given them. Separated from his cares by the oblitterite, James drifted immediately off to sleep. Jerome did, too.

CHAPTER 33

The Road to Epiphany

IN THE MORNING James was awakened by insistent loud knocking. He stumbled to the door. "Mayor Culpa!" James cried.

Hearing the goat's name, everyone burst from their beds and ran to greet the little scapegoat, smothering him with hugs.

"I'm so-oorrry," he said sheepishly. "You were all having such a good time, I felt useless and sorry for *myself*."

"*I'm* sorry, Mayor Culpa," James said. "It was my fault for—"

"Baa-aa-aahh!" the little goat snapped back, stamping the ground. "Stop it! I momentarily forgot what I was bred for, that's all. *I'm* to blame! Let's get that straight once and for all!"

He got so worked up that he snorted and shook, then took a running leap at the nearest wall. *BANG!* And with that everything was back to normal.

With their group reunited, James asked Jerome and Marie to step outside while Culpa and Kiljoy argued the merits of their exploits so far and when to return to Average. Roget refereed.

"So what about it?" James began. "Come back with me. We'll find your father."

Marie was ready to give her father another chance, but Jerome stubbornly refused.

"I'm never going back! I will never be like him."

"But you *are* like him," James pleaded. "You're so much like your father! You both have a temper, and you're—"

"Average?" Jerome finished James's sentence scornfully. "Is that what you were going to say?" He said it as if it was the worst insult he ever heard.

"What's so wrong with being average?! Most people are!" James argued.

Jerome stormed back into the cabin, slamming the door. James threw up his arms in defeat.

"Why don't you go back yourself?" Marie suggested. "We'll be all right. We'll make our own way."

"But *where*?" Then it struck. "Wait a minute," James cried, punching his fist in the air. "Epiphany! I know how to get there!" He pulled his shirt collar aside, revealing the rolled map.

Marie was wide-eyed. "Where did you get it?"

"I can't tell you. But we need to get Jerome to Epiphany. It's better than a good idea. He'll find his destiny! And I'm betting it includes you and your father."

James ran into the cabin and began to pack. "Let's go."

Within the hour the five companions were ready. A glumly resigned Kiljoy spent the time writing out his last will and testament inside Roget's pocket. They set out and bade farewell to Gus, Faith, Hope, and all the rest of the crew of the Eureka Mining Co., who wished them luck and with sadness watched them head for the impossible.

James caught the eye of Slim Chance, the cockeyed man who had given him the map, and waved. Slim waved back, putting his finger to his lips.

When they were out of sight of the camp, James took out the map.

"Here's Eureka," James said, pointing to a spot on the map. "We started walking this way."

His finger traced a dotted line from where they were to a spot between two mountain peaks labeled Mt. Deception and Mt. Perception. The line ended at a point called The Leap of Faith.

"Epiphany has to be here," said James. "At The Leap of Faith. Let's go."

CHAPTER 34

The Leap of Faith

THEY STOOD HIGH on a ledge between the sheer cliffs of Deception and Perception. Far below, a cluster of round structures with thatched roofs nestled on the canyon floor.

"There it is: Epiphany," announced James.

It was a dizzying drop and there was no way down.

"Too bad," Kiljoy announced. "Let's go home."

James picked up a rock and threw it down at the huts to alert the inhabitants of their presence. In only half a second, the rock made a loud crack against the rock wall behind the huts. Not only did it not take as long as he expected to fall the distance, but the resounding noise it made as it hit the ground sounded very nearby. *Strange,* James thought.

Throwing the stone worked. Two tiny figures emerged from two of the huts far below.

"Hello!" James hollered, loudly.

"Hello," replied a soft voice. It sounded very close, startling everyone.

"Can you help us?" James hollered down again.

"Can... you... show... us a way... down? Down there!" he pointed.

"No need to shout," the voice said softly.

Again everyone on the ledge spun around. It sounded as if the person speaking was standing right next to them.

James decided to speak as quietly as the voice did as a test and gently asked, "Can you show us a way down?"

"Jump," replied the voice.

"Jump?!" screamed Kiljoy. "It's a thousand feet to the bottom!"

It looked at least that far from atop the cliff. The two tiny figures looked up at them and waved.

"It's not as far as you think," the voice told them.

Kiljoy shimmied up Roget's lapel and grabbed him by the collar. "Don't you dare believe him!" he commanded.

Roget turned to James. "I agree with Kiljoy, my demi-king. Not advisable."

"Listen to him! LISTEN TO HIM!" begged Kiljoy.

Jerome and Marie moved cautiously to the edge and looked down.

"No way!" said Jerome.

"But that's Epiphany down there," said James.

"You can't be serious," Jerome said. "Look how far down it is!"

Marie arched her brow, puzzled for a moment. Then before anyone could react, she took hold of Jerome's hand and stepped off the ledge, yanking Jerome over with her. It happened in a split second.

James, Roget, and Culpa screamed, "Nooooooo!" reacting spontaneously by simultaneously reaching out for the twins, losing their balance and falling forward.

There was no time to scream on the way down. They instantly hit the ground and tumbled over one another as if they had fallen off a short step. Which they had.

"Ohmygosh! That was scary," said James, his heart hammering in his chest.

Roget got up and dusted himself off. He deftly replaced the bowler atop his head, regaining his composure. "'Zere! You see? Not so bad. *N'est-ce pas, mon ami*? I should 'ave known!" he said, peering into his vest pocket. "Ha, ha! Look at 'zat, Kiljoy 'as fainted. Heh, heh, heh." Then, without warning, all the color drained from Roget's face and he keeled over.

James and Marie fanned Roget to revive him. The two figures they had seen from above now stood next to them. They were monks in saffron-colored robes. Both had large tattoos (*Or were they birthmarks?* James wondered) in the shape of a question mark on the tops of their shaved heads.

"Welcome to Epiphany," said one of the monks. "We are Epiphanums. My name is Wu-Pe and this is Yee- Ha."

"Come," said Yee-Ha. "You must have many questions."

Too many, thought James, but now was no time to think about Average. Not before his friend found his destiny.

CHAPTER 35

Yee-Ha and Wu-Pe

YEE-HA AND WU-PE led everyone to one of the smaller circular yurts on either side of a larger one. The walls of the yurts were made of thick, heavy fabric and hide stitched around a frame of sticks. This one was spare inside, neat and clean. A bamboo sleeping mat and blanket were near the wall. In the center was a brazier with a warm glowing fire. Smoke smelling of incense rose up through a hole in the roof.

"Jerome has an important question," James volunteered.

"Oh?" Yee-Ha said to James. "And you do not?"

"Oh, yes. But I can't ask. I'm not supposed to."

"Why?" the monk asked.

"I'm to be King of Average, and I'm not supposed to know too much. That would disqualify me."

"I see," the monk said, casting a glance at Wu-Pe.

"Why did you come?" Wu-Pe inquired.

James pointed to Jerome. "For my friend."

Yee-Ha handed out small bowls of steaming hot tea. The tea was delicious; it was more sweet than bitter, and spicy, too.

Jerome spoke up. "I need to know what I should do with my life. I need advice, I guess you'd say."

Wu-Pe asked, "You came for guidance, then?"

"Yes," Jerome agreed. "Guidance."

The monks nodded.

"And you?" Yee-Ha turned to Marie. "You are here because…?"

"Because of my brother," said Marie.

"And, if he finds what he is looking for. What then? What is it you want?"

"I shall be very happy if he is happy," she said with a laugh.

Wu-Pe leaned in. "You are not happy now?"

"No, I *am* happy now and I'm very glad to be here. I know I'll be fine whatever I decide to do. I just haven't given it much thought." She laughed her lovely laugh and James smiled.

Wu-Pe nodded. "Maybe now you will."

"Maybe," said Marie.

Yee-Ha noticed the amulet around Jerome's neck.

"What is around your neck?"

"It's a Presence Stone. It makes you… It gives you presence of mind."

"And does it?" asked the monk. "Does it give you peace in this moment?"

Jerome had to think about that. James paid careful attention.

"It felt like it did, back in Serenity," Jerome said.

He considered it a moment longer and said, "No. I feel restless. Like I should be doing something else. Something more important."

"More important than being here? Now?"

"Yes," Jerome answered. "I look toward the future but I don't know what I want. That disturbs me."

"The stone does not help you, then?"

"I guess not. Not anymore," Jerome allowed.

"Then it is a stone around your neck and nothing more. Perhaps you should discard it."

Jerome took it from around his neck and waited a moment to feel a change. "I don't feel any different with it on or off."

"Ah! Just so," Wu-Pe said. "Perhaps it might do some good for another seeker."

"From me to you," Jerome said, handing James the amulet. "A present. I hope it works for you like it did for me back in Serenity."

"Thank you," said James, deeply touched. He hadn't expected this. In fact, he'd never gotten anything like a gift before ever in his life. His mother never celebrated his birthday or had any kind of party for him. Even Christmas was just another day to play in his room and let his mother have her peace. Nobody he could remember had ever given him any sort of present. A lump rose in his throat. "I-I..." Tears came and he couldn't stop them. He made his way outside, embarrassed by this sudden outpouring of emotion.

Everyone followed him out into the sunlight. "Why do you cry?" Yee-Ha asked.

Culpa had been waiting outside, grazing on the supply of thatch straw that was used to patch the yurt's roof.

"Ja-aa-mes! Whatever it is, it's my fault! Baaa-aah! Kick me! Go ahead! Kick me. You'll feel better!"

James got himself under control and dried his eyes. "No. I'm fine, Mayor. It's nobody's fault. I'm just a crybaby, that's all."

The two Epiphanums exchanged knowing looks. Jerome asked them, "Is that it then? Or do you have more advice?"

The monks burst out laughing. "We have not yet begun."

Wu-Pe took Jerome around the shoulder. "Come, you must be very hungry. Let us eat. We have much to discuss." He led Jerome toward the other small yurt on the far side of the central one.

Marie fell in step with her brother when Yee-Ha called to her. "Please, I would be honored if you would be *my* guest and join me," he said, motioning to the yurt they had just come from. "I will give you something to eat as well and we will talk."

Marie nodded, but stopped. She and Jerome both said simultaneously, "What about James?"

"It's okay. Roget and I will wait for you here!" said James, smiling and waving.

"*Oui! Bonne chance!* Good luck!" added Roget.

"Baa-aaa-ah!" said Culpa between chews.

"Never mind me," said Kiljoy, obviously hurt. "Go on, then. Just one thing," he called. "I wouldn't trust them if I were you!"

Jerome and Marie exchanged anxious looks, but nonetheless, each disappeared into the Epiphanums' yurts.

"*Excusez-moi,* my demi-king," whispered Roget. "I must 'ave a little talk with my friend. 'E feels neglected. I will be back." Roget walked around behind the central yurt talking solicitously to Kiljoy.

James squatted down and gave Culpa an affectionate pat.

"It won't be long now." His stomach rumbled.

"There is food in here, if you are hungry," a rich and somehow familiar voice came from within the yurt. "Will you join me?"

James hesitated.

Culpa assured James he'd be fine munching on thatch and urged James to get something to eat.

"Come in," the voice repeated.

The wooden door to the big yurt swung open.

Because the sun was high in the sky, James could see only darkness within. But then he saw a dim light flicker, and an enticing aroma wafted out. James was uneasy and he didn't know why. He debated whether to remain outside or satisfy his hunger. His hunger won out and he cautiously stepped inside.

CHAPTER 36

Ah-Ha

THE YURT LOOKED even bigger on the inside. Rectangular panels of colorful fabric set out a few feet from the round walls formed an inner sanctum. They were intricately embroidered with hundreds of beautiful question marks and exclamation points stitched in gold and silver.

Seated on cushions surrounding a glowing brazier sat another Epiphanum. He wore the same style robe as Yee-Ha and Wu-Pe and sat cross-legged on a small mat. His head was bowed in meditation. Tattooed on the top of his head was a light blue question mark.

"Sit."

James settled himself across from the monk on some soft pillows.

The man raised his head slowly. His face was familiar.

"Do I know you?" James asked.

"You do," replied the monk. "I am you."

James laughed. "No, you're not. *I'm* me."

The monk laughed. "I am Ah-Ha, High Epiphanum. I am a seer and a mystic. A magician, too. I can be anything I choose to be. We all can. And here, now, in this moment, I choose to be you—you! As a fully grown man."

"You do look like what I might look like, all grown up," James allowed.

"Ah-Ha!" he exclaimed. "Just so. My voice sounds familiar too, yes? Like the voice you hear in your head, does it not?" The monk smiled. "I propose this. Let us consider what sort of man you will grow up to be. As you are now, on your current path, imagine I am your future. I am King of Average. Ask me anything you like. I will do my best to answer. 'What it is like to be king? What duties must you perform? How must you act?' Anything. 'Will you be a good king, loved by all?' Ask. I will tell."

"But I can't. If I know too much…"

"You won't be average?" the monk said, finishing James's thought. "Perhaps. Or maybe that's just what you have *chosen* to believe. Belief is power."

"No, that's not it. Um, Ah-Ha, sir," James politely corrected the monk. "I was specifically told not to ask too many questions or I couldn't be king."

"Do you believe *everything* you're told?"

James considered this: he remembered the Nervous Nellies, who believed whatever they were told, and the Ninnies, who believed everything they were told as well; he remembered Culpa's warning about being a know-it-all and the judges' admonition and Norman's mandate.

"I shouldn't, should I?" James answered. "I mean, I don't want to be a Nellie or a Ninny, but I suppose I'm…" James searched for the right word. *Too trusting? Gullible? Naïve?*

"And what of the questions you would *like* to ask, but mustn't? You have put much out of your mind, haven't you?"

It was hard to think. Was it because he had given half his idea to that miner in Eureka?

"I don't know how to explain it," James said. "I just wanted to be the most average person ever so I can... so I could..."

"Be a good boy. And make everyone *like* you?" the monk probed. "Is that it?"

James conjured the pitiful image of Alistair the Vainglorious, King of the Ninnies, begging and pleading for them to keep his secret.

"You've done that, haven't you? You've been obedient, kind, and helpful. You saved King Norman. You came here to help your friends find their way back to him. You are a good boy. An *especially* good boy."

Another voice replied in his head. *Be careful*, it warned. *Don't listen to this*, it added. It was more of a threat than a warning.

"Thank you," said James, forcing a smile, resisting the voice, which was growing louder and more insistent.

"I think you have chosen this way because you believe you are not likeable as you are. That you are not worthy of love," Ah-Ha concluded.

James recalled how pitiful and terrified Alistair looked as he lied about the most ridiculous things, trying to fool everyone into loving him. He had fooled no one but the Ninnies. He was pathetic. Was James just as pathetic, making everyone believe he wasn't?

"Because, dear James, if everyone knew what you knew, they'd detest you as you much as your mother detests you. And, be honest, as much as you detest yourself," said a very different voice. James's whole body trembled with fear.

"Do you think everyone is stupid? Do you think I am stupid, you worthless little boy?! We all can see what you truly are."

The words sent an electric shock up James's spine. His hair stood on end.

"You *are* nothing!" James watched Ah-Ha dissolve into the Shadow. The face was dark, featureless, and transparent.

James's heart constricted and his insides curdled. He was frozen with overwhelming terror. He couldn't breathe.

"Isn't that the truth, dear James?" the malevolent Shadow asked in a sincere tone. "The dark secret you hide? That special knowledge you and I share?"

James heard the ring of truth and pressed his hands to his ears and shook his head. "I don't know what you mean," he said weakly.

The robes deflated to the mat. The Shadow slithered toward him like a vile black liquid spilling onto the floor. When it reached him, it seeped through his pant legs and latched onto his skin, stretching onto the floor and taking on the form of his own little-boy silhouette, distinctly visible by the light of the fire. It stared up at him, moving now as he moved.

"You lie!" it hissed. "You're nothing! You are a worthless, good-for-nothing mistake of a child who ruins lives!" Its mocking, derisive laughter was horrifying. "*Nobody* loves you! Nobody *can* love you. You don't deserve it. You can't even love yourself! And do you know why no one will ever love you? Just because, James! Just because you are who you are!"

James wasn't aware he was hunched over, beating his fists on the floor. "Look into your heart, James! You hate who you are almost as much as everyone else does. As everyone must! It's the truth! Isn't it? The truth, James! THE TRUTH!"

Yes, it was true! He couldn't shut it out. He was exposed at last!

Then, from somewhere deep inside his soul, in a place unknown even to him, an unnamed truth he had no words for flickered like a small candle in the cavernous abyss of his dark fears. He frantically focused on that tiny flame and reached for it. As he did, the flame leapt higher. When he touched it, it flared into fury.

"NO!" James shouted. "It's not true! I've tried to be good. I have! I have to be good for *something*!" He could hardly see through his tears.

"Even *you* don't believe what you're saying, you pathetic, miserable little boy! ADMIT IT!" it snarled.

A cold breeze chilled him with this command.

The flame went out. His angry outburst spent, James sobbed uncontrollably. "I'm not so bad! I'm *not*!"

The Shadow expanded and spread across the floor, engulfing him in terrifying darkness. "You ARE that bad! You are *worse* than bad! You deserve NOTHING!"

The Shadow was becoming more opaque and now James was becoming less distinct, barely visible.

"Yes, nothing," James whimpered. Then with vehemence, he shouted, "I SHOULD NEVER HAVE BEEN BORN! I never should have… Ahhhh!" He gave way and began to dissolve into the Shadow.

Suddenly there was a crash. Monsieur Roget, bound and gagged, had kicked one of the panels to the floor. He lay with a tiny bulge in his pocket writhing, punching, and screaming for help. James reached out from the darkness toward his friends. He heard loud thwacks as Culpa rammed the door.

The Shadow's voice barraged him with more negativity, growing louder and louder. It was deafening!

Another panel fell to the floor, revealing the little blackbird with orange-tipped wings trapped in a cage. It madly flew against the bars, trying to escape. Another panel fell, revealing his mother caught in the Nellies' thorny net. "You did this to me! You destroyed my life! I'm trapped and it's all your fault!"

His neighbors, classmates, teachers, and even strangers he'd never met stepped out from behind the other panels, advancing on him and leering at him in horror and disgust.

James was reeling, caught in a maelstrom of his worst nightmares. He whirled around and around.

Everywhere he turned, he saw contempt and loathing on everyone's face as they recoiled at the very sight of him.

But the one person who didn't recoil was Monsieur Roget, lying prostrate on the ground. His eyes pleaded with James to free him. He was shrinking!

James forgot everything else and ran to Roget, but as he tried to untie him, Kiljoy escaped from the optimist's pocket and ballooned up into an ogre. The Shadow funneled into the giant pessimist, as if Kiljoy was a vacuum cleaner sucking up the darkness.

The huge pessimist stood over the quickly dwindling optimist and lifted his foot, ready to squash Roget out of existence.

CHAPTER 37

The Horns of Dilemma

MAYOR CULPA BURST through the door, scattering splinters everywhere. The Monster Kiljoy hesitated slightly as James dove for the tiny optimist, snatching him away from certain death, and pocketed him just as Roget would have done for the old Kiljoy.

The valiant scapegoat banged repeatedly into the ogre's shins. Kiljoy let out a howl and grew even larger with every strike, his pinched face contorted in pain.

Then, before James's eyes, Kiljoy transformed from a horrific giant pessimist into an enormous snorting minotaur with lethal pointed horns. The creature bellowed and pawed the ground, lowering its head, ready to charge.

Culpa lowered his head, and he and the apparition raced at each other.

James screamed, "Nooooo!"

But it was too late. They collided sharply. Crack! The little goat was no match for the raging bull-headed creature, and Culpa collapsed.

Outraged, horrified, and forgetting his fear completely, James leapt at the huge brute and grabbed it by the horns. The creature struggled, but James wrestled it to the ground and found the strength to hold it down. It snorted and grunted in fierce bursts. James held fast.

Then suddenly it ceased struggling and relaxed. It spoke to James in a terrifyingly seductive voice, "Good for you. You've won. You have me in your power, James. I am yours to command."

James's arms trembled from exertion as he kept a firm hold on the horns.

"See there?" it said. "Your little friend was no match for me. He couldn't protect you but I can. I'm powerful. Our rage can destroy anyone who dares try to get near us," the creature said. "Let me protect you. I want to serve you."

James's nerves and emotions were stretched piano-wire tight. What should he do? Master this beast and have it shield him from everyone's hatred? Or help the little scapegoat who had guided him and chided him into this bizarre, wondrous world? Was it already too late?

Culpa lay on his side, his chest heaving up and down unsteadily. The little goat managed to lift his head. "James! It's NOT... YOUR... FA-A-ault!"

Culpa's eyes closed, and his chest stopped its erratic spasms. He lay still.

James let go of the horns, forgetting everything else, and held the stricken goat in his arms.

"Mayor Culpa! Please!" he wailed. "It's my fault! All my fault! I made it happen. I did this. I'm sorry. I'm sorry, I'm sorry! I am so sorry!" But the brave little scapegoat didn't respond.

"He was weak. I am strong. I'll keep you safe," whispered the beast, still prone, lying calmly next to the motionless Culpa. "He took your guilt. I'll give you power! Together we can destroy all those who blame you—those who hate you! We will crush them."

White-hot anger surged through every fiber of James's being and his rage multiplied on a quantum scale until he exploded with a sound that shook the walls. It was a howling scream beyond rage; a long- suffering wail of pain and sorrow tore from his throat.

He flung himself at the creature and as he dove, the horrid thing evaporated and James fell forward into the pillows before the fire.

James lay sprawled, an empty husk, too weak and spent even to push himself up onto the pillows. He was numb. All his feelings were frozen in suspended animation like bubbles in ice.

The room was now bathed in a soft light, and the sweet aroma of food and incense once more filled the air. Ah-Ha, the monk, was seated on his mat, quietly meditating, looking nothing like James or the man he was to become. He was a smiling, wizened old man with laughing eyes and a kind smile. The pale blue question mark on the top of his head was now a bright blue exclamation point. The Shadow was gone. The images of horrified people were gone, too, as was the pessimist-ogre-minotaur. And Roget was no longer in James's pocket. The visions were so real. Or were they? But there lay Culpa beside him, lifeless on the floor.

"Come," said Ah-Ha softly. The Epiphanum gently lifted him up and guided him to the door. James didn't resist, couldn't resist. He stood up zombie-like and stepped out of the yurt and into blinding, dazzling daylight.

CHAPTER 38

Aftermath

"JAMES! JAMES!" It was Marie's voice. She sounded very far away, yet here she was with her arms around him, giving him a warm hug. "Isn't it wonderful?"

She buried her head in James's shoulder, crying tears of joy. Her hair was soft against his cheek. She smelled sweet and fresh, but he saw, heard, and felt her from a thousand miles away.

"James? What's the matter?"

Whether he couldn't answer or didn't want to answer didn't matter. He was silent.

Roget and Jerome gathered around them.

"What is 'ze matter?" Roget asked.

Ah-Ha looked on compassionately and kept a supportive hand on James's shoulder.

James registered everyone's concern but couldn't react. He swallowed, noticing his throat was raw from screaming. Roget was right in front of him with Kiljoy peeking cautiously out from the Roget's pocket.

"He has had a great struggle with powerful forces to reach his epiphany," Ah-Ha explained.

Roget noticed the broken door on the yurt and ran to look inside. "*Mon Dieu!* It is Mayor Culpa! Come everyone, please come quick!" he shouted, disappearing into the yurt.

Marie and Jerome raced into the yurt. James watched, still detached.

"It was a deep wound," he heard Ah-Ha tell Ye-Ha and Wu-Pe. "A hole in his soul covered by a thick armor of ignorance, very hard to pierce. He is truly a remarkable boy."

James didn't flinch at the compliment. Words meant nothing to him.

"You must rest now," Ah-Ha said in a gentle voice. The three monks led James to Ye-Ha's yurt, laid him down on the mat, and covered him with a soft blanket. Wu-Pe placed a leafy bundle of Serenity vines on the fire. James watched the smoke rise from the tendrils and waft overhead in delicate wisps. Ah-Ha and the other Epiphanums backed out slowly, bowing respectfully as they went. The door closed as James let blessed sleep overtake him.

CHAPTER 39

Compassion

JAMES OPENED HIS EYES expecting to see the walls of the yurt and the cone-shaped ceiling above him. But he was out in the open air, resting on a red-and-white checkered picnic blanket spread out on green grass. The sun was shining, and the sky was a beautiful shade of blue. In the distance he heard the laughter of children at play.

I know where I am, James thought. I'm back in the real world, in Dean Street Park near my house.

James rose and headed toward the happy sounds, to a small patch of blacktop asphalt surrounded by a tall chain-link fence. This was the playground where he'd sometimes go after school. There were children climbing the jungle gym, and two boys played tetherball. Several smaller kids were on the steel roundabout, a heavy metal disk of a merry-go-round with hand-holds on its outer rim.

James remembered how much fun it was to watch the world whirl around and around from the roundabout, then hop off and fall onto the grass to watch the sky spin above him, as if he was the center of the universe.

He returned to the picnic blanket and saw a girl about his own age seated on it, waiting for him. She wore a frayed, stained white jumper. Her raven-black hair was tied back with a piece of red yarn, and her skin was very fair. She had pretty, downcast dark brown eyes. She was shy, unable to look at him.

James knelt beside her. She held a rose stem in her fingers, having picked all the petals from it. They were strewn about on her lap. Now she was picking the green shiny leaves from the thorny stem, tearing off each leaf deliberately, one at a time.

"What's the matter?" he said.

"Nobody loves me," she said. "I'm all by myself."

"Nobody?"

She nodded. "Every time I get something of my own, my brothers take it away. They get everything. They beat me and tease me."

"Why don't you tell your parents?" asked James.

"Momma won't believe me. She only loves my brothers. They take all my things and lie to her. She hates me. They all hate me. No one ever wants to play with just me! By myself," she said, jabbing her finger angrily at her chest. "I'm not important. They don't even know I'm alive."

"How many brothers do you have?" he asked.

"Nine. I'm the youngest. I'm in the way, just another mouth to feed. That's what Momma says."

"But a mother should love all her children," James said, trying to comfort her, wishing it was true, and sadly knowing it wasn't.

"Not her!" said the girl. "She never even sees me. No one will ever give me a single thing I want. If you want something, you have to take it for yourself. Nobody will do it for you."

"What about your father?" James asked.

"My brothers threw him out of the house a long time ago. Momma made them." The girl picked the last leaf of the stem and tore it into little pieces. "He's a good-for-nothing bum, she says. All men are. My brothers are too, that's what I think. All boys are horrid. They make my life miserable."

A tingle of recognition ran up his spine and James realized whom he was speaking to: this little girl would grow up to be his mother. One day, these words would be her words. Knowledge like this often happens in dreams; some things you just know.

"Are you so sure that *no one* loves you?" he asked.

"Yes," she said.

"It's not true. I love you. I will always love you." James awoke with a start.

CHAPTER 40

Grace and No Blame

WITH A SUDDEN INTAKE of breath, James was back in the yurt. The sweet smell of Serenity vine permeated the air. Above, the center hole of the cone-shaped roof let the rays of the sun stream in through the fragrant smoke in golden streaks. He propped himself up on an elbow to get his bearings. That's when James noticed he wasn't alone. He felt something soft and warm snuggled up against him.

"Mayor Culpa!" shouted James incredulously. He threw his arms around the goat's neck and buried his face in his soft fur. "Oh, Mayor Culpa. I am so sorry. I am so, so sorry." James couldn't help saying it, he was so happy.

"You should be-e-ee," said the goat. "Hmmph! Putting me through all that! You're sorry? I should say so!"

James was astounded "What?!" He sat bolt upright. "What are you saying?"

"I'm saying, apology accepted." The goat got up on all fours and shook himself out to fluff up his matted fur.

"You have nothing on," James observed. He had never before seen Culpa without his green tweed vest and spectacles. "What happened?"

"What ha-a-aa-ppened?!" bleated the goat. "My goodness, James, I thought you'd be more perceptive than that! Perhaps you're only average after all."

"You're not a scapegoat anymore, are you?" he asked.

"That's better!" said the goat, doing an about-face and trotting out the door.

"Wait!" James moved to follow the goat out but stopped abruptly.

He was aware of a new sensation. Wonderful wasn't the right word, although it was close. He felt… well, the only words that could describe it were *reborn; brand new; whole.*

Once again, everything had changed in a flicker of an instant. But this time the world hadn't changed as much as he had. James made his way outside.

Jerome and Marie stepped up behind him.

"Hi," Jerome said with a smile so wide it threatened to bend his ears back on his head.

"Good morning, James," said Marie with an exhilarating look of admiration and happiness. She hugged him tightly.

"And 'ow are we 'zis fine day?" Roget strode up, monocle in place, walking stick clicking, his bowler perched jauntily on his head. He grabbed James by the shoulders for the traditional smooch on both cheeks. James replied in kind.

"Brother!" moaned Kiljoy in his usual dour manner. "Give it a rest!"

"How am I? I'm… *magnifique!*" exclaimed James. "*Très bien!* Very good, my friend."

The pretense was gone. James felt incredibly himself. He was who he truly was, the person he had made himself to be. He was comfortable in his own skin for the first time in his life and it fit like a glove. Gone was the infectious sway of the Shadow. Gone was the "nice boy" routine and the constant fear of being exposed as an impostor. He was genuinely who he was: a decent person, and a very clever one at that, capable of anything he could imagine.

"And you?" James asked hopefully. "Did you have... did you get your...?"

"We did!" the twins exclaimed at the same time. James looked around. The sheer cliffs below The Leap of Faith were gone. He was much higher up. "Is this still Epiphany?"

James looked back at the familiar yurt he had emerged from and it vanished with a gust of wind as they all looked on.

"*Non*, my demi-king, we 'ave risen above it!" Roget laughed. "It is truly amazing!"

He walked James over to the lookout. The sheer cliffs of Mount Deception and Perception were far below. They stood on a wide promontory of the tallest peak—Mount Impossible. The air was thin and chilly and the view was spectacular.

In the distance James saw the blue surface of Lake Superior glittering in the sunlight and the rolling landscape of all the territories he'd passed through. From here they were smooth and green. There was the Mighty Meander and the River Maunder bisecting the countryside. On the other side were Average and Median City. Beyond that he could just make out Inferior and the Sea of Doubt, shrouded in a gray-blue haze at the rim of the horizon. *So this is Mount Impossible,* James thought. He smiled and hollered, "I hereby dub thee MOUNT POSSIBLE!" His voice echoed through the canyons, "*POSSIBLE... OSSIBLE... ssible...*"

"We're way above Average, aren't we?" said James.

"That we are," said Norman, stepping down from a sturdy rope secured farther up the mountain. His tattered blue tunic was replaced with a rugged hide coat lined with fur. The former king's white hair was pulled back behind his ears and a weathered oilskin broad- brimmed hat topped his head.

James's heart pounded joyously in his chest.

"I was going to find *you* and bring Jerome and Marie back with me!" James said. "How did you find *us*?"

"Wrraaawk!" the familiar squawk of the little bird resounded off the hard faces of the formerly Unattainable Mountains.

"A little bird told you?" James laughed.

"How did you guess?" said Norman, laughing. He strode across the ledge to James and his children and gathered the three of them in his arms.

Among the many sensations and new experiences James had experienced in the Realm of Possibilities, this warm embrace was by far the best. Folded in the arms of this father and his children and scrunched between his first best friend and Marie, James felt that he was a welcome part of something. *This is family,* he thought. It's what he had always longed for, but it was also bittersweet.

The image of his poor mother, alone, bitter, and unhappy appeared in his mind. He knew, at last, that it wasn't his fault, but it still made him sad.

"Oh, James," Marie sighed. "We were so worried when you came out of Ah-Ha's yurt."

James was silent, recalling the horror of confronting the Shadow.

Jerome spoke. "Thank you, James. Without you we would never have gotten this far. And never realized..." His chin quivered. Jerome was on the verge of tears. "How much we loved our father."

James nodded and gave Jerome's shoulder a squeeze.

"You gave me back what I valued most, James. My children," Norman said.

"Average will be the better for having you all back as a family," said James.

Kiljoy sprang from Roget's pocket like a grouchy grasshopper, landing on James's collar. He complained loudly in his ear, "So now you're not going through with it? All this trouble and you won't be King of Average after all? I thought so!"

"Enough!" Roget declared, forcibly plucking Kiljoy from James's shirt and stuffing him roughly into his pocket. "You will not spoil this. It is too 'appy a moment!"

"We're not going back to Average," Norman stated flatly.

James was astonished. "What? Why not?"

"You should know better than anyone," Norman answered.

"You changed our world," said Marie.

"I did? How?"

"That's a very good question," said Norman, with a knowing grin. "Maybe you'll find the answer to that someday."

"I believe I will," said James, laughing loudly.

Everyone joined in, except for Kiljoy, who stewed contentedly in his own misery.

"James, you're welcome to come with us. We're going to explore these mountains. There's lots to see and I want to show my family what is possible."

Family, thought James. *I'm part of a normal family at last.*

CHAPTER 41

To Thine Own Self Be True

JAMES BEAMED at his new friends. They beamed right back. *A brother and sister*, thought James. *And a father to look up to.* His heart was bursting with happiness.

"I'd love to come with you," James announced. Marie gave a shout of happiness and Jerome nodded his approval to James with a broad grin, his eyes shining with joy.

Norman looked down at the three still in his embrace and said to James, "That's wonderful, son. I'm glad."

"Thank you, Da—. Er, sir." James felt a brief moment of awkwardness. He'd wanted to call the former king "Dad," but it didn't sound right somehow. Norman released them and stood up to survey the horizon and the surrounding peaks.

"Where shall we head first? Perhaps over the summit and down; I'm sure there's something grand for us to see."

Roget strode up to James and placed both hands on his shoulders. "I am 'appy for you, *mon ami.*" He drew James close to plant yet another set of kisses on James's cheeks but James drew back on impulse.

"I'm sorry, I can't."

"What?" said Kiljoy, popping out of Roget's pocket, eyes wide with disbelief and sudden interest. All eyes turned to James.

"My mother needs me." He watched his friends' happiness evaporate and felt sad, but certain. "I have to go home."

"But wha-a-aat about us?" Culpa asked.

"*Mais, oui!*" Roget implored. "We 'ave all come so far together. To separate now would be, for me—un*think*able!"

"Speak for yourself!" shouted Kiljoy.

Everyone became solemn.

"Do you have to go?" Marie asked.

She took James's hands in hers and looked so disappointed that James was ready to reconsider just to make everyone happy, especially her. *But,* he thought, *I'd be doing what someone else wants instead of what I know I need to do.* Of all that he'd learned, he understood that above all, he had to be true to himself.

"Wraawk!" The little bird sprang into the air in a flurry of black and orange feathers and shot past them, flying high above the tallest peak that was once Mount Impossible. He disappeared down the other side.

James brightened and turned to Norman and his children and his friend the optimist.

"Would you like to see where I live?" James asked. "I want to introduce you to my mom. She's been so unhappy for so long. I think we could do something very important for her."

Kiljoy spoke up. "That's crazy! Look at us!" he said, indicating the dapper Frenchman from his perch in his vest pocket. "We'd scare the living daylights out of her and she'd probably attack us!"

"I think you're partly right, Kiljoy," James laughed.

"Roget will definitely scare her, but somehow I think you two will get along just fine."

"What will you say to her, *mon ami*?" Roget asked.

"That I love her, and I always will, no matter what." Kiljoy moaned.

"I don't really know what she'll do, and I know she won't believe me, but that's what I'm going to say anyway."

"If she won't believe you, why bother?" challenged Kiljoy.

"Quiet, you little pest! Always 'ze wet blanket. Maybe one day you shall convince her, *mon ami*. Always there is hope."

"Anything is possible," said James. "So you'll come with me?"

Without hesitation, they all agreed. Even Kiljoy relented.

"Another adventure!" proclaimed Roget. "'Ow marvelous!"

'Ze End

About the Author

ORIGINALLY FROM New York State, Gary Schwartz began his professional career as a mime at age 13, performing up and down the Hudson River with Pete Seeger and the great folk entertainers of the 1960s.

In the 1980s, he appeared in numerous film and television projects, including the Oscar-winning feature film *Quest for Fire*. As a voice-over artist, he's lent his voice to hundreds of film and television projects and is the voice of several well-known video game characters, including Heavy Weapons Guy and Demoman in *Team Fortress 2*.

Schwartz has written for two children's television series in which he co-starred: *Zoobilee Zoo* as Bravo Fox and the Disney Channel's *You and Me, Kid*.

Gary studied with and became the protégé of Viola Spolin, the creator of Theater Games, the basis for improvisational theater in America. He is a passionate dynamic improv coach and facilitator devoted to carrying on Spolin's techniques.

The King of Average is his first novel.

Learn more at www.gary-schwartz.com.

About the Illustrator

NICOLE ARMITAGE IS an illustrator with projects spanning theme park attraction posters, signs, and children's books.

Her portfolio and contact information can be found at www.armitagearts.com.

Acknowledgments

I WOULD LIKE TO THANK Susan Hughes for her very thorough notes and questions—she was a great mentor and helped me shape the story and improve my writing. To Eva Moon, who pointed out the need to balance the female perspective and fixed a lot of faulty typing. Thanks, also, Wendy & Joe Wahman and Mark Brandon for his comments and corrections.

Thank you to Christina Lepre, who's done a great job of editing and made the book so polished. To Tricia Parker, who proofread this more than once and to Gwen Gades for the lovely cover design. Thanks also to Pam Labbe for her input.

Added thanks goes to Mark Breitfuss for challenging me to show him 30 pages in 30 days and, in doing so, allowed me to end up with a whole book.

To my pal, Stan Brothers, who gave me some space to write at his home in California I want to say "Thanks for the use of the hall."

To Norton Juster and his book *The Phantom Tollbooth*, thanks for inspiring me as a child. I now wish to do the same for others with this volume.

Thank you to Vanya Drumchiyska who's done a great layout job, making it into its present form.

And to my wife, Tina Brandon, for most everything else.

CPSIA information can be obtained
at www.ICGtesting.com
Printed in the USA
LVOW12s1627050717
540359LV00002B/368/P